ADVENTURES IN SPACE

The architecture of science-fiction

By Jon Jardine with an introduction by Neil Baxter

Illustrated by Ian Stuart Campbell, Douglas Prince, Ciana Pullen and Piotr Sell

First published 2016 by
The Royal Incorporation of Architects in Scotland

Text
Jon Jardine, Neil Baxter Hon FRIAS

Illustrations
Large colour-treated cityscapes by Ian Stuart Campbell
All other illustrations Douglas Prince, Ciana Pullen and Piotr Sell

Design
Jon Jardine (mail@jonjardine.com)
Typeset using Futura and Eurostile Extended

Cover
Piotr Sell
Inspired by the striking art of Frank R Paul and the San Francisco of *Star Trek*

ISBN 978-1-873190-74-6

A catalogue record for this book is available from the British Library.

*This book and the accompanying exhibition are part of the Festival of Architecture 2016,
a key event in Scotland's 2016 Year of Innovation, Architecture and Design.*

Supported by

 EventScotland

CONTENTS

"By 'scientifiction' I mean the Jules Verne, HG Wells and Edgar Allan Poe type of story — a charming romance intermingled with scientific fact and prophetic vision."

Hugo Gernsback
"A New Sort of Magazine"
Amazing Stories
Vol 1, No 1, April 1926

PREFACE

Shaping Scotland, the strategy for the UK's most ambitious ever, year-long, national celebration of architecture, was published in 2014. Its authors, Eleanor McAllister OBE and Stuart MacDonald OBE envisaged that the Festival of Architecture 2016 would celebrate the contribution of architects to our quality of life, engage with audiences across Scotland and generate unique events with international appeal.

Among Stuart MacDonald's particular contributions to the strategy for the Festival was his vision of an exhibition on the cross currents between science-fiction and architecture. This innovative exhibition at Glasgow's Lighthouse, of which he was founding Director, would, in Stuart's words "offer insights into the architecture of science fiction" and "engage the popular imagination".

Sadly Stuart did not live to see his vision fulfilled. His sudden death, in early June 2016, came just weeks before the launch of *Adventures in Space*. That exhibition and this publication testify to Stuart's enduring influence as an inspired curator and educationalist.

Spanning nearly 200 years and over 150 books, comic books and movies, this review is a comprehensive chronological exploration of science-fiction. Jon Jardine's selection of highlights spans from Mary Shelley's *Frankenstein* (1818) to Ridley Scott's *The Martian* (2015). The drawings which richly illustrate the five themes, by Ian Stuart Campbell and an inspired group of young European artists, lend coherence to this disparate, intriguing and inspiring list. Inarguably the genre which has most influenced the evolution of our built environment, science-fiction continues to inspire new generations of architects to 'boldly go…'!

David Dunbar PPRIAS
Chair
Festival of Architecture 2016

INTRODUCTION:
STAR GAZERS, SKYSCRAPERS AND FLIGHTS TO THE MOON

Over its 200 year history, science-fiction has held a mirror to rapidly accelerating technological change, shared fears, an architectural and urban revolution and evolving geo-political realities. Roughly contemporaneous with the emergence of science-fiction as a distinct genre, has been a radical change in the way buildings are built and consequently the form of cities across the globe.

The moving image, the medium whereby much science-fiction storytelling has been communicated to a mass audience, emerged as a new art form in the final years of the nineteenth century. It arrived in nice time to promulgate the prophetic, scientific and extra-terrestrial visions for which the writer Hugo Gernsback would coin the phrase "scientifiction".

The movies came along at a time when new forms of mass entertainment were required to address the new demands arising from increased leisure time. A gradually more egalitarian, less labour intensive, more equal, society opened up opportunities for time off in evenings, weekends and holidays. From Louis le Prince's earliest filmic explorations, frame by frame, in 1888 on a bridge in Leeds, via steam trains entering stations, Georges Méliès' fantastical flights to the moon, to *E.T.* and *The Martian* a century later, the new medium was well suited to tell extraordinary stories.

Movies also opened up new horizons, both feeding and encouraging new aspirations among their audience. Arguably too, by sharing imaginative ideas about futuristic gadgets, gizmos and modes of transport which might, in time, become real inventions, they also helped catalyse technological advances.

The same changes in society which helped spawn science-fiction and the movies would also prove transformative in architecture and urban form. Historic, hand-hewn, stone-on-stone traditional building, reliant on plentiful, cheap labour which had formed the towns and cities of the past, would, over time, be rendered obsolete by machine technology and new, less labour intensive, methods of building.

Indulgent decoration would, in the early decades of the twentieth century be eclipsed by a new consideration of how buildings might appear if new techniques were taken to their logical conclusion. Steel and concrete structural frames freed up facades and the evolution of the elevator enabled buildings and cities to rise, quite literally, to new heights.

All this technological progression also coincided with improvements in general and specialist education and increasing aspirations in western society. What had been exotic and out of reach became, if not commonplace, at least accessible.

By the latter part of the twentieth century, previously undiscovered territories would be just a budget flight away and the world's horizons were narrowed. Whereas the fiction of the past had described quite unfamiliar and thereby intriguing, terrestrial experiences, science-fiction tapped into a desire for more extreme exploration. Of all popular fictional genres, science-fiction and fantasy, the latter arguably a revisiting of long established fairytale traditions, are the most escapist.

What, after all, could be more removed from most folk's day-to-day reality than journeys into the future, encounters with space aliens or apocalyptic visions of dystopian dictatorships? Science-fiction novels, comics, TV and, most particularly, film, often commented on familiar themes but in very unfamiliar settings. Film, immersive and powerful in its embrace of the viewer, provided immediate and easy access to these new narratives.

Film is also, of course, a shared urban phenomenon. The population shifts, which had supported the increasing heavy industrialisation of the nineteenth century, continued throughout the twentieth as patterns of work changed. The dawn of the current millennium coincided with one of the most significant moments in human history. In the early twenty-first century for the first time, more people on planet earth were city dwellers than lived in the countryside. The shift from agrarian to urban had reached a fundamental tipping point.

Western industrialisation pre-dates the emergence of science-fiction by several decades. However, the move from handcraft to machine made, the evolution of new techniques and materials, the freeing up of building facades from structural function and the growth upwards of the high rise city, are all reflected in the fictional works of artists and filmmakers. Many of these works envisaged the further progression of the changes which were happening around them – and often they didn't like what they saw.

Credit for writing the first science-fiction novel is usually given to Mary Shelley for *Frankenstein* which was published in 1818. However, it wasn't until nearly half a century later that the first of Jules Verne's series of fantastical exploration novels was published. Some 30 more years were to pass, until

HG Wells and others produced works which truly commenced the continuous evolution of science-fiction which can be traced right through to the present day. Thus it is arguable that the three cross cutting evolutions of architecture, science-fiction and, by association, film itself which are traced in this book are even more contemporaneous than might at first be imagined.

Frankenstein was a one-off. Usually categorised under "Gothic Horror", it drew upon rich themes which preoccupied the early nineteenth century. However, the means by which Dr Frankenstein's creature is brought to life are technological. Thus, the deserving plaudits to Mary Shelley for the first important work of science-fiction.

Mary Shelley's work reflected the contemporary fascination with electricity, a long known about phenomenon but only relatively recently (1791) acknowledged as the medium by which neurons pass signals to muscles. While Frankenstein was therefore an acknowledgement of scientific discovery in human biology, both Verne and Wells' works were more responsive to the extraordinary pace of industrial and technological change in the second half of the nineteenth century. Their works consolidated the genre in a series of novels exploring new territories – the centre of the earth, the depths of the oceans, outer space and perhaps boldest of all, the future.

While early works of science-fiction reflected the ever increasing pace of change in science and technology, the settings of these early novels and the first science-fiction films were often less futuristic. The built environment of these early novels was decidedly of its era. Later filmmakers would make great play of the anachronism of futuristic technologies amid settings awash with decorative Victoriana. This reached its apotheosis in Alan Moore's *The League of Extraordinary Gentlemen* comic book series and the subsequent (2003) film of the same name, directed by Stephen Norrington.

Of course, anachronism is not restricted to the movies. There are many early photographs of starkly linear prototype modernist buildings with an incongruous, open-topped, vintage tourer parked outside. The buildings may be of the future but motor car streamlining wasn't moving at quite the same pace.

Inarguably the key moment in terms of the depiction of the city in science-fiction was the first visit of the Austrian filmmaker, Fritz Lang, to New York in October 1924. Reflecting on that visit later, his overwhelming emotion seems to have been anxiety. In the footage that survives from Lang's 1927 masterpiece, *Metropolis*, that anxiety is reflected in the above and below ground cities which divide the moneyed elite from the subterranean slave class. The journey of the protagonist to visit his powerful father in the "new tower of Babel" added elevated highways and airborne urban transport to a cityscape that was otherwise recognisably contemporary New York.

The Futurists, particularly Antonio Sant'Elia, in Italy and the Russian Constructivists had published their own fantastical visions of a densely populated urban future. Le Corbusier's collection of polemical essays, *Vers une Architecture*, from 1923, proposed a new architecture stripped of decoration, optimising, in Corb's view, the potential of the structural frame in freeing the external appearance of buildings from superfluous decoration.

Subsequently, Corb's design for a *Ville Radieuse* (translated into English as 'The Radiant City') took up the same theme, expanded to city scale. Like Fritz Lang, both Sant'Elia and Corb saw transport links between and among their great edifices as crucial to the workings of their respective variants on the modernist metropolis.

Meanwhile, in tandem with the progression of science-fiction and advances in structural framed architecture, film technology was also progressing rapidly. Early black and white depictions of street scenes and everyday events evolved, via silent melodramas and slapstick comedies, often played out against a live Wurlitzer organ soundtrack. New, more nuanced, styles of acting, developed for in front of the camera.

Although pioneering "natural colour" footage was produced as early as 1902, most films were hand-coloured until the advent of the "talkies" in 1927, somewhat paradoxically, resulted in a reversion to black and white. Various natural colour processes emerged in the late 1930s but it wasn't until over two decades later that colour became the norm. So, in the first half century of sci-fi movies, the future often tended to be monochrome.

Perhaps understandably, given the cost of creating movie sets on an urban scale, movie makers have tended to use existing buildings and cities to depict the future or even other worlds. Just as *Metropolis* had built upon New York, Frank Lloyd Wright's late works played bit-parts in several movies. The Greater London Council's brutalist Thamesmead South housing estate contributed to the sense of oppression of Kubrick's *A Clockwork Orange* (1971) and Buckminster Fuller's geodesic domes provided the limits of the horizon in *Logan's Run* (1976).

The next great evolution of cities in sci-fi film arrived with arguably the most significant change in movie making techniques of the late twentieth century, Computer Generated Imagery (CGI). Films like George Lucas' *Star Wars – The Phantom Menace* (1999), Roland Emmerich's *The Day After Tomorrow* (2004) and, of course, *Inception*, directed by Christopher Nolan from 2010, where Paris literally folds in on itself, made the most of the new opportunities which CGI proffered.

It wasn't until the late 1930s, when Dorothy set off toward the Emerald City in glorious Technicolour that (more or less) natural colour started to become more of a feature in the movies. The same year witnessed the ultimate expression of a future where automobiles and highways in the sky were the catalyst to transforming urban form. Norman Bel Geddes' world of tomorrow, *Futurama* at the New York's World's Fair in 1939, would be the last great visionary utopia before the cataclysm of the Second World War.

Thus, for a brief moment, as the movies looked to a brighter tomorrow and a shining city, inspired by science-fiction, was proposed as a potential urban future, all the portents seemed positive. As EB White observed of his visit to Bel Geddes' diorama,

"I didn't want to wake up. I liked 1960 in purple light, going a hundred miles an hour around impossible turns ever onwards towards the certified cities of the flawless future."

Alas, much reality became truly dystopian in the years immediately after 1939. The War would, of course, set the scene for future themes for science-fiction movie makers, of distorted and damaged cities, oppressive regimes and the horrors of the atomic bomb.

Over the decades which followed, aliens were set to become more monstrous and sci-fi visions of urban apocalypse would steadily increase. However, as the first great era of science-fiction has demonstrated, the future has a habit, through time, of becoming the past. Human habitations have tended, over time, to improve and there's always room for optimism. After all, as the first century and a quarter of the film industry would have us believe, the hero usually wins.

Neil Baxter
November 2016

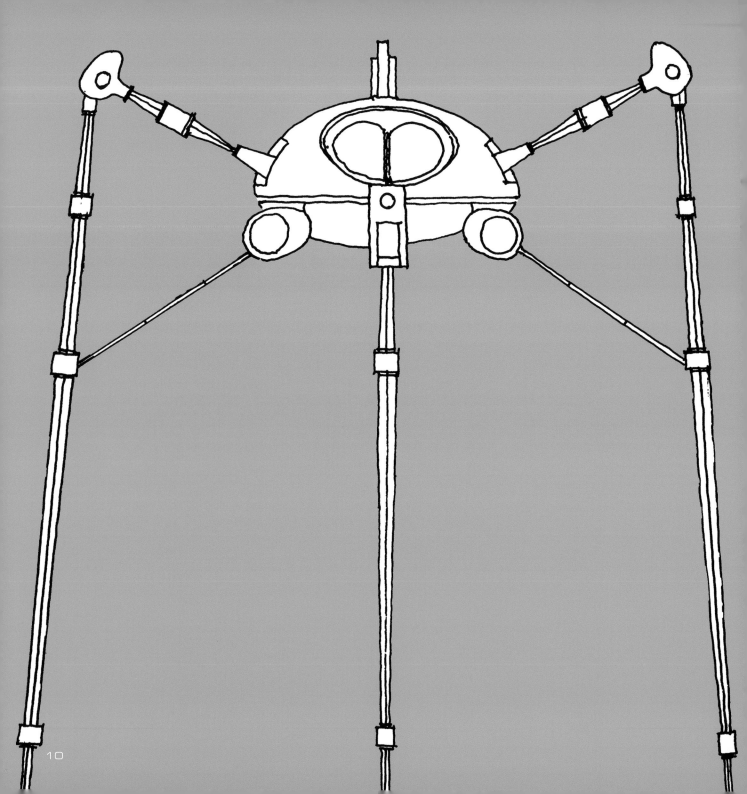

EARLY VISIONARIES

The beginning of the nineteenth century saw what many claim is the first true work of science-fiction – Mary Shelley's chilling first novel *Frankenstein*. The rapid industrialisation of the nineteenth century and the dawning of new technologies including electricity, the telegraph and powered transportation encouraged 'scientific romances' from other visionary writers including Jules Verne and Herbert George (HG) Wells.

The start of the twentieth century and the dawn of cinema brought new pioneers, trailblazing French film director Georges Méliès used special effects to invent tales of travelling into space. New construction techniques, innovations in materials and the invention of the elevator allowed architects to build more complex and taller structures. The centre of cities, especially in the United States, became denser and more vertical.

The concepts of the Italian Futurists, just before the outbreak of the First World War, further inspired the next generation of visionaries to imagine ever-more elaborate worlds.

1818

Frankenstein; or, The Modern Prometheus
Mary Shelley

Victor Frankenstein's resurrectionist experiments bring to life a hideous, powerful but sensitive being – with horrific consequences. The nineteen-year-old Mary Shelley brought together themes from horror stories, tales of doomed romance and the exploration of morals from the Gothic tradition with science as the foundation of her narrative.

Frankenstein brings his creature into being by harnessing electricity. In the context of the age the power that animated lightning bolts was still a great mystery to most.

1864

Journey to the Centre of the Earth
Jules Verne

A scientific expedition ventures underground through the crater of an extinct volcano to discover a vast ocean, populated by prehistoric animals. Verne's later works would draw more on contemporary science.

The novel has been filmed on a number of occasions, including in 1959 (dir. Henry Levin) and 2008 (dir. Eric Brevig).

1865

From the Earth to the Moon
Jules Verne

An American gun club builds a giant cannon, to launch a projectile to the moon.

Verne attempted some calculations for the technical requirements for the cannon. Despite the lack of any data, some of his results are close to what would be required for a real moon launch.

This novel, along with HG Wells' *The First Men in the Moon*, inspired the 1902 film *A Trip to the Moon* (dir. Georges Méliès). The story was adapted again in 1958 (dir. Byron Haskin).

1895

The Time Machine
HG Wells

An English scientist travels into the far future and discovers two dystopian societies of light and dark facets of humanity living on a dying planet Earth. The novel reflects Wells' socialist views and the contemporary challenges of industrial society.

The most influential time-travel story of all, Wells' novel has been adapted many times, most famously in the 1960 film (dir. George Pal). The film won an Oscar for its time-lapse effects which mapped social and, to a lesser extent architectural, evolution as the hero travelled into the future.

1870

Twenty Thousand Leagues Under the Sea
Jules Verne

A group set out to hunt a sea monster which has been attacking shipping but turns out to be a very advanced submarine, owned by Captain Nemo.

Verne was inspired by the very primitive submersibles developed during the American Civil War. Descriptions of Nemo's ship, the *Nautilus*, accurately predict features on submarines far into the future.

The 'twenty thousand leagues' refers to the distance travelled, rather than the depth.

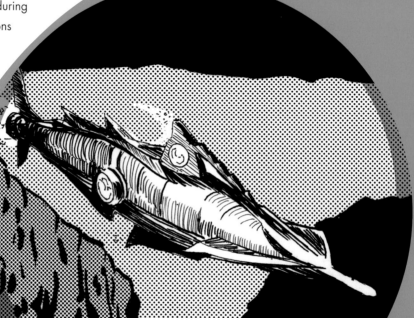

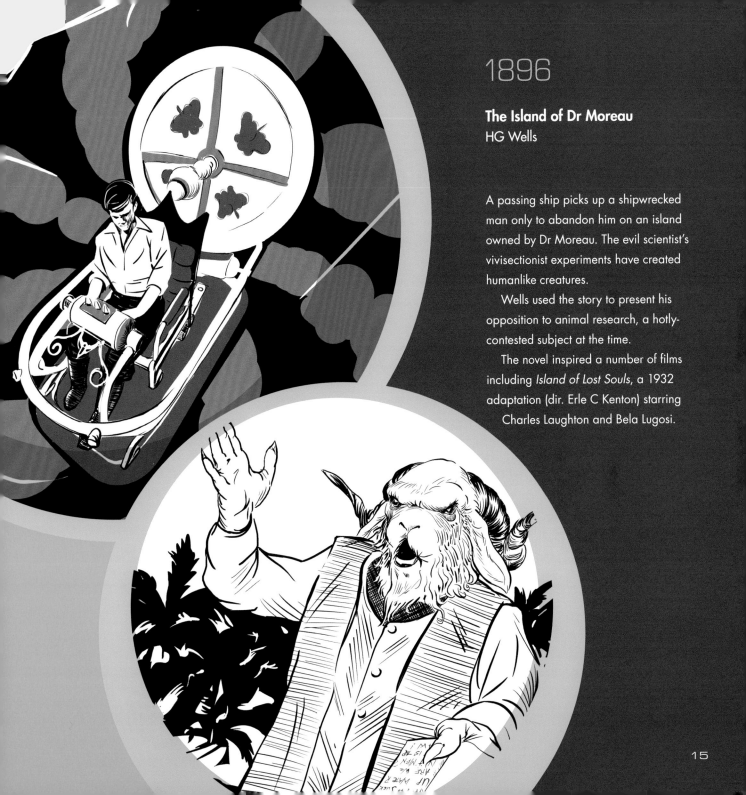

1896

The Island of Dr Moreau
HG Wells

A passing ship picks up a shipwrecked man only to abandon him on an island owned by Dr Moreau. The evil scientist's vivisectionist experiments have created humanlike creatures.

Wells used the story to present his opposition to animal research, a hotly-contested subject at the time.

The novel inspired a number of films including *Island of Lost Souls*, a 1932 adaptation (dir. Erle C Kenton) starring Charles Laughton and Bela Lugosi.

High Rise Construction

Traditional building techniques, with loadbearing external walls, restricted the height of buildings and for centuries dictated the form of towns and cities. The evolution of concrete and steel structural frames and the invention of the elevator enabled architects and engineers to design much taller structures.

The late nineteenth century United States was among the first to embrace this new high rise technology and the form of cities began to change radically with buildings soaring ever upwards.

Chicago mercantile blocks inspired New York skyscrapers. In due course Europe followed suit and in major industrial cities, like Glasgow, ten story office buildings, previously unthinkable, became the norm.

Home Insurance Building, Chicago
William Le Baron Jenney, 1884

Flatiron Building (originally Fuller Building), New York
Daniel Burnham, 1902

Woolworth Building, New York
Cass Gilbert, 1913

1898

The War of the Worlds
HG Wells

Victorian England is invaded by the Martians using tripod fighting machines with advanced weaponry. Humanity is only saved when the Martians are destroyed by bacteria to which the invaders have no immunity.

The novel dramatised concerns about growing international tensions, with an alien force attacking Britain in a similar manner to the Imperial British domination of other nations through superior technology.

The novel has been adapted on numerous occasions, including Orson Welles' radio broadcast of 1938, which treated the story as 'rolling news', causing mass panic in the United States. Jeff Wayne's musical version from 1978 brought Wells' story to a whole new audience.

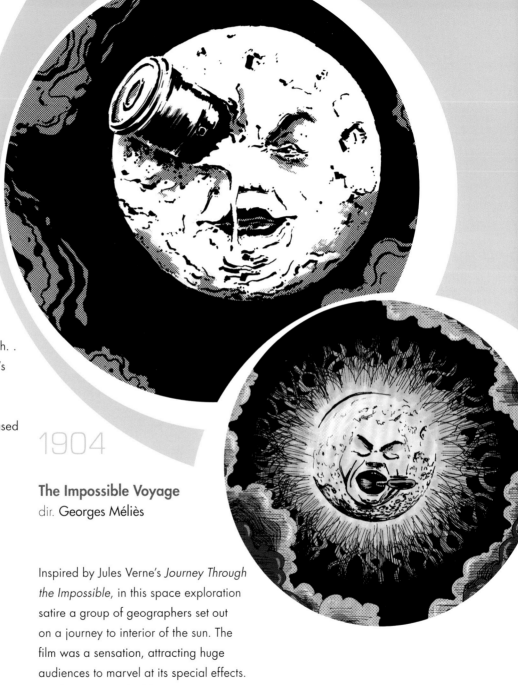

1902

A Trip to the Moon
dir. Georges Méliès

Jules Verne and HG Wells had created an appetite for space exploration fiction. In this film the protagonists journey to the moon in a spaceship fired from a giant cannon. They narrowly escape from the underground-dwelling inhabitants, one of whom they capture before returning to Earth. .

Internationally successful, the film's lavish production values, innovative effects and long running time were hugely influential. The film was released in both black and white and colour versions, the latter with every frame laboriously tinted by hand.

1904

The Impossible Voyage
dir. Georges Méliès

Inspired by Jules Verne's *Journey Through the Impossible,* in this space exploration satire a group of geographers set out on a journey to interior of the sun. The film was a sensation, attracting huge audiences to marvel at its special effects.

Like *A Trip to the Moon,* some prints of the film were hand-coloured.

1911

Ralph 124C 41+
Hugo Gernsback

Not known for its literary merit, this novel is renowned for its many accurate technological predictions, including television, tape recorders, solar energy and radar (along with some notable 'misses').

Gernsback was an inventor, writer, editor and magazine publisher. His later contributions to the genre are so significant that he is sometimes referred to as "The Father of Science Fiction". The World Science Fiction Convention Awards, the "Hugos", are named in his honour.

1912

John Carter of Mars
Edgar Rice Burroughs

The hero of Burrough's 'Barsoom' (Mars) series, the immortal John Carter, first appeared in the pulp magazine *The All-Story*. The first novel from the serials, *A Princess of Mars*, was published in 1917, after Burrough's *Tarzan* series was successful and is regarded as a classic of 20th century pulp fiction.

The subject of many comic book treatments in the decates since his first appearance, John Carter has also been the distinctly Tarzan-esque looking hero of a number of movies. The influence of the character on subsequent heroes, including Flash Gordon and Superman has been acknowledged.

The director of the 2009 science-fiction epic *Avatar*, James Cameron, cites John Carter of Mars as inspiring his own 'boys own' story.

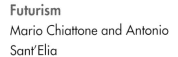

Futurism
Mario Chiattone and Antonio Sant'Elia

Born in early twentieth century Italy, Futurism envisaged the future of humanity as densely urban. The Futurists rejected history and the movement's leaders, including architects Mario Chiattone and Antonio Sant'Elia, proposed utopian visions in two seminal series of drawings: *Buildings for a Modern Metropolis* and *Città Nuova.*

Futurism

They envisaged that new technologies would free buildings from internal load-bearing walls. Their designs for soaring, narrow skyscrapers with thin facades were shocking to older generations who still saw the Renaissance as the model of architectural perfection. More worrying still in these visionary futures, external elevators soar skywards and viaducts bridge great urban chasms, hundreds of metres in the air.

The Futurist emphasis on speed was expressed in bold predictions of streamlined trains and planes. Sant'Elia's written predictions for a future of urban towers and fast transport were edited by Marinetti who published the *Futurist Manifesto* in 1914. These early architectural forays were more about rebellion than reality. Pictorial imaginings took precedence over any realistic design. Sant'Elia died in the First World War in 1916 and Chiattone's architecture developed in other directions. Their Futurist visions were never built.

PULP FICTION TO THE 'GOLDEN AGE'

The coming of age of science-fiction saw the transition from 1920's 'pulp' simple narratives to the 'golden age of science-fiction' from the later 1930s to the post-Second World War era.

Many of the same authors started their careers with short stories or novellas in comic-books or science-fiction magazines before progressing to more ambitious narrative formats.

Stories often followed the earlier formula of adventures set on alien planets with simple adversarial 'cowboys vs indians' narratives.

As the medium evolved, magazines sought more layered and credible, science-based, stories with more rounded characterisation. Substantial and complex novels began to emerge and the movies followed suit.

This progression of science-fiction narratives reflected both demand on the part of an increasingly sophisticated and mature audience and the skills of the writers themselves. New novels challenged the ingenuity of their authors as the genre shifted from storybook to more literary aspirations.

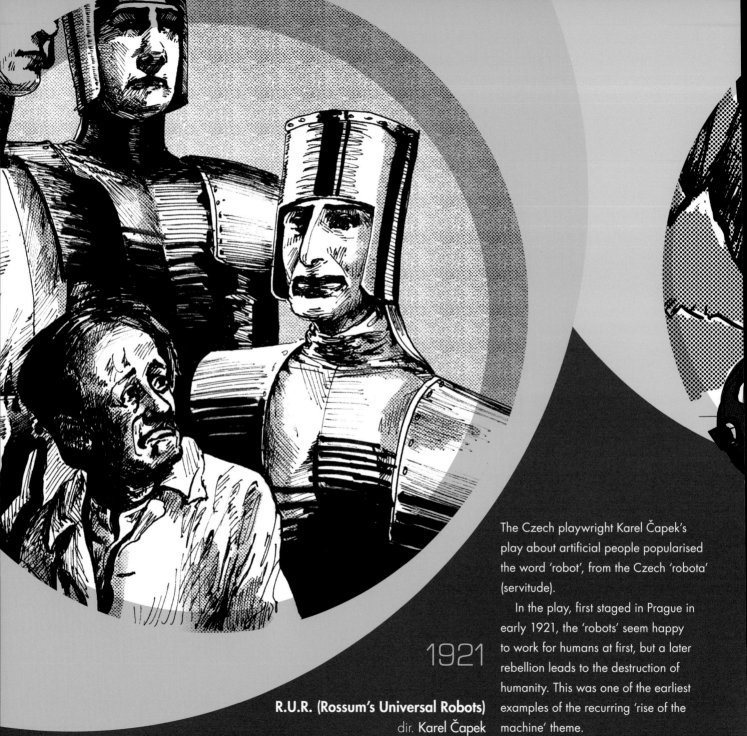

1921

R.U.R. (Rossum's Universal Robots)
dir. Karel Čapek

The Czech playwright Karel Čapek's play about artificial people popularised the word 'robot', from the Czech 'robota' (servitude).

In the play, first staged in Prague in early 1921, the 'robots' seem happy to work for humans at first, but a later rebellion leads to the destruction of humanity. This was one of the earliest examples of the recurring 'rise of the machine' theme.

Amazing Stories

The world's first dedicated science-fiction magazine was founded in New York by Hugo Gernsback. The cover artist was Frank R Paul, whose work, in bright, garish colours, would go on to characterise the style of the whole pulp genre.

Gernsback wanted his magazine to be educational. However, *Amazing Stories*' readership was more concerned with escapist adventure. Authors whose first work was published in the magazine include Isaac Asimov, Ursula K Le Guin and Roger Zelazny.

Towards an Architecture
Le Corbusier (1887–1965)

The publication, in 1923, of *Vers une Architecture* by the Swiss architect and polemicist Charles-Edouard Jeanneret (known as Le Corbusier or 'Corb') was a key moment for the modern movement in architecture. Known in English as *Towards a New Architecture*, Corb's collections of essays recognised that technological advances enabled the creation not of buildings which looked the same but were built differently, but of a whole new industrial architecture.

In this new style of architecture form would follow function, echoing the famous phrase by the American architect, Louis Sullivan. Corb's book, considered by many as the single most influential work on modernism, created a huge stir. Architecture was irrevocably changed.

Frank Lloyd Wright
(1867–1959)

The prolific and innovative architect Frank Lloyd Wright is widely acclaimed as the greatest American architect of all time. His early houses in his native Chicago combined clean lines with geometric detailing and open plans.

As Wright's reputation grew so did the scale of his commissions, including important commercial and industrial developments. Wright's late works borrow from the sci-fi imagery of the era and in their turn, influenced the genre.

Ennis House, Los Angeles
Frank Lloyd Wright, 1924

Johnson Wax Headquarters, Racine, Wisconsin
Frank Lloyd Wright, 1939

Studio Building, Dessau
Walter Gropius, 1926

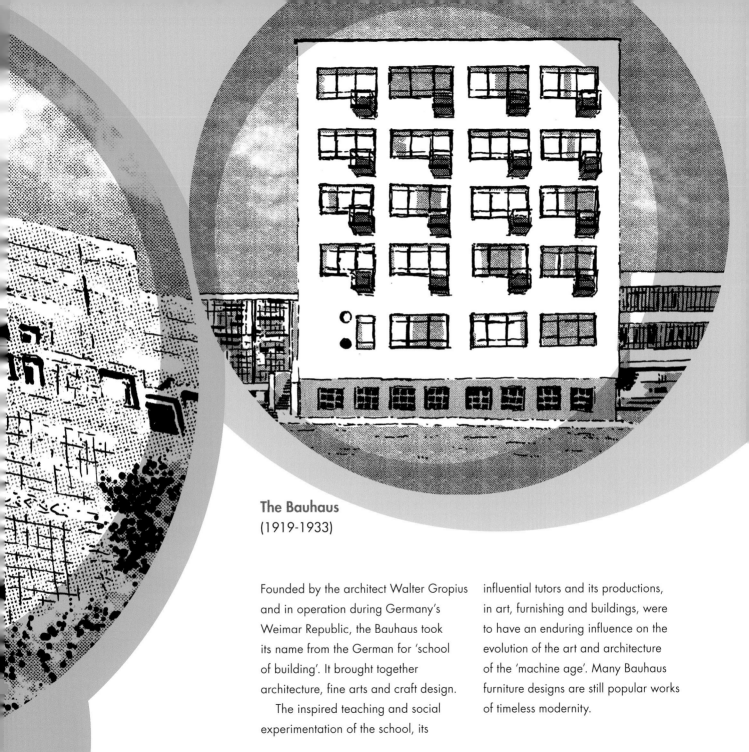

The Bauhaus
(1919-1933)

Founded by the architect Walter Gropius and in operation during Germany's Weimar Republic, the Bauhaus took its name from the German for 'school of building'. It brought together architecture, fine arts and craft design.

The inspired teaching and social experimentation of the school, its influential tutors and its productions, in art, furnishing and buildings, were to have an enduring influence on the evolution of the art and architecture of the 'machine age'. Many Bauhaus furniture designs are still popular works of timeless modernity.

1927

Metropolis
dir. **Fritz Lang**

The wealthy industrial elite reigns from mighty skyscrapers, whilst the worker class struggle in horrendous conditions below. The city of Metropolis itself is arguably the main star of the film. Its design was influenced by New York skyscrapers and Deco Moderne, one of the most fashionable architectural styles of the time.

Metropolis

Metropolis became the architectural template for all future cities in cinema, with towering skyscrapers connected by bridges and elevated highways. The streets below are crowded with people, swarming like ants.

The futuristic, modernist, Art Deco mega-city of Metropolis warned of what could come of unchecked expansion and industrialisation. The seemingly utopian city ultimately becomes a dystopian, dehumanising nightmare.

"Metropolis … was born from my first sight of the skyscrapers of New York in October 1924… I thought that it was the crossroads of multiple and confused human forces, blinded and knocking into one another, in an irresistible desire for exploitation, and living in perpetual anxiety."

Fritz Lang

1929

High Treason
dir. Maurice Elvey

Set in a futuristic London of
1940 (changed to 1950 in
later releases), war is looming
between continental superpowers,
the Empire of Atlantic States and
the United States of Europe. A city
of monumental buildings is heavily
influenced by *Metropolis*.

    The theme reflected the post
First World War fear of the
technological super-state,
accurately anticipating
future political
realities. Meanwhile
flying machines
pass by
overhead.

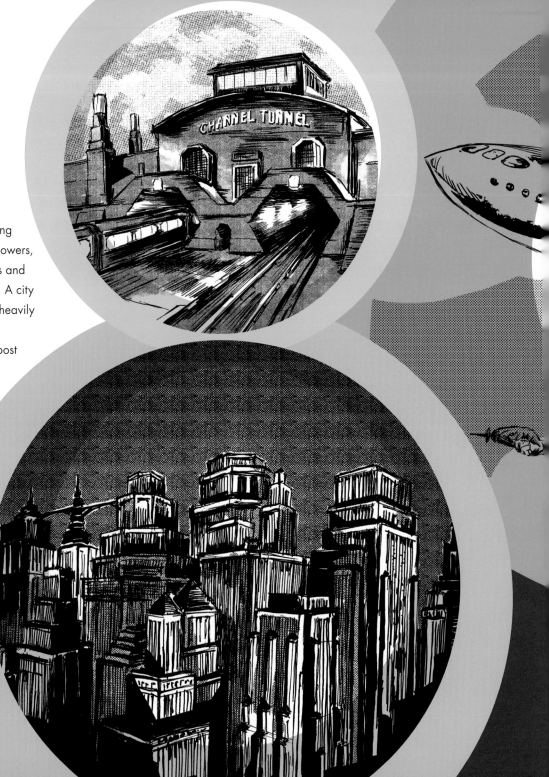

Buck Rogers in the 25th Century
Philip Francis Nowlan

First published as a newspaper comic strip, based on a novella from the previous year, *Armageddon 2419 AD*, Rogers is exposed to radioactive gas while investigating unusual phenomena in an abandoned mine. He falls into a state of suspended animation and awakens in 2419…

The popularity of the Buck Rogers strips inspired others, most famously Flash Gordon. Buck Rogers later appeared on radio from 1932, in film and on television in 1950 and 1979.

1930

Astounding Stories of Super-Science

The world's oldest, continually-published, science-fiction magazine had more high-profile pulp authors than *Amazing Stories*, due to paying higher fees to contributors.

Authors published over the decades include Isaac Asimov, Ray Bradbury, Arthur C Clarke, Philip K Dick, Robert Heinlein, Anne McCaffery, Lois McMaster Bujold, Larry Niven and Frederik Pohl.

It has changed its name on a number of occasions, and is now *Analog Science Fiction and Fact*.

1930

Just Imagine
dir. David Butler

This musical comedy, the first sci-fi 'talkie', depicted a futuristic New York in 1980. Like *Metropolis*, its Art Deco-styled, Manhattan had massive skyscrapers, soaring ever upward, connected by suspension bridges and multi-lane elevated highways.

Although it was a financial flop, it provided clips of the imaginary New York of the future to other fantasy adventure films, including *Flash Gordon* and *Buck Rogers*, earning back some of its huge cost.

Intourist Garage, Moscow
Konstantin Melnikov, 1933

Narkomitiazhprom, Moscow
Vesnin Brothers, 1934

Rusakov Workers' Club, Moscow
Konstantin Melnikov, 1928

40

Constructivism
(1913–1935)

The first phase of Constructivism originated in Russia, led by Vladimir Tatlin. The theoretical basis of this artistic revolution was that art should serve a social purpose. Effectively it was the antithesis of previous aesthetic art movements. Constructivism had a major influence on architecture, both in Russia and through the progressive German (Bauhaus) and Dutch (De Stijl) schools. It also influenced graphic design, theatre and fashion There was a split in what had been a fairly unified Constructivist grouping in 1922 and a number of different factions went on to pursue what each considered the true spirit of the movement.

1932

Brave New World
Aldous Huxley

In Huxley's dystopia, human embryos are conditioned to belong to one of five castes. The 'alphas' are destined to be leaders and the 'epsilons', stunted and stupefied, to become menial labourers.

Huxley set out to parody HG Wells' utopian visions of the future. His 'negative utopia' used the settings and characters to express widely-held fears of losing individual identity in a fast-paced future. The novel predicted developments in reproduction, sleep-learning and psychological conditioning.

Le Corbusier
1887 – 1965

The most influential architect of the twentieth century, Le Corbusier, sought to utilise machine production to create his ideal city of the future. His early house designs featured long ranges of windows and rectangular planes of reinforced concrete.

His urban plans, a response to the overcrowded squalor of Paris, envisaged skyscraper housing and steel-framed office blocks with glass-curtain walling. As well as public transport hubs and fanciful airports in the sky, 'Corb' saw the motor car as an opportunity to liberate the citizens of this utopia.

**Ville Radieuse
(Radiant City)**
Le Corbusier, 1930

1936

Flash Gordon
dir. Frederick Stephani

The thirteen-episode film serial *Flash Gordon* tells the story of Flash's first visit in his rocket-ship to planet Mongo and his confrontation there with the evil Ming the Merciless. The character had debuted in newspaper comic strips just two years before.

The 1980 version (dir. Mike Hodge), with a soundtrack by Queen, saw Brian Blessed deliver a characteristically bombastic performance as Prince Vultan. Its opening sequence, strangely, was shot on the Isle of Skye.

1936

Things to Come
dir. William Cameron Menzies

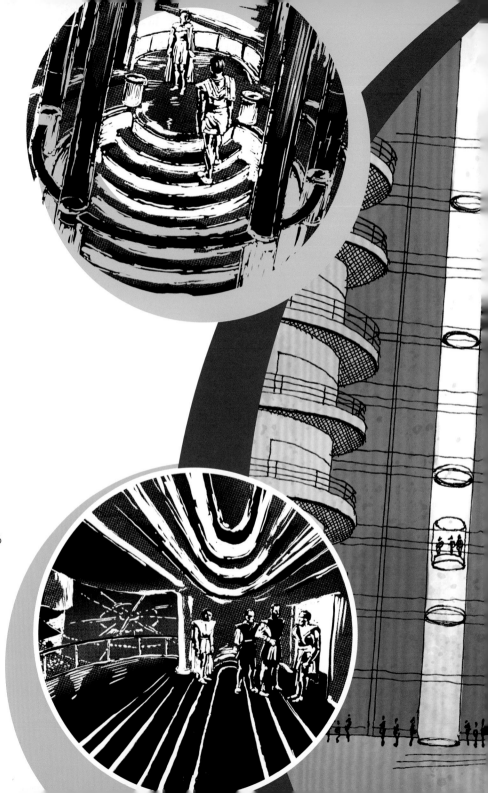

With a screenplay by HG Wells, from his novel *The Shape of Things to Come*, the film is an alternative history of the world in the future, from 1940 to 2036. A global war starts on Christmas day in 1940, eventually leading to the survivors living in a subterranean world carved out beneath the ruins of the uninhabitable cities above.

Wells disliked *Metropolis'* vision of workers as oppressed brutes, exploited by a managerial elite. The film emphasises Wells' belief in a technocratic society.

Vincent Korda, the production designer, approached Le Corbusier to design the sets, but he declined. Korda's fellow Hungarian émigré, László Moholy-Nagy, then living in London, was commissioned.

The sets feature curved atria, criss-crossed by sky bridges, with elevators in glass tubes rising through them. They are at once abstract yet reminiscent of Le Corbusier and Ludwig Mies van der Rohe, two of Moholy-Nagy's former colleagues at the Bauhaus in Germany.

1939

The World of Tomorrow
1939 World's Fair, New York

General Motors' *Futurama* at the New York World's Fair was designed by Norman Bel Geddes. The massive installation envisaged the world twenty years into the future. The Futurama urban landscape was composed of entirely modern architecture, interspersed with huge industrial plants.

Expressways connected the nation with steady traffic connecting cities, surburbia and the countryside. The one-acre sized model included more than half-a-million individually-designed buildings and fifty-thousand cars.

Conveyors carried passengers across Bel Geddes' vision of a lush landscape punctuated by his utopian 1960s visionary cities. Although Europe was on the brink of a war into which the USA would also be propelled, for the brief interlude of the World's Fair the future looked bright.

Futurama, the largest-ever physical model of an imaginary time to come, where the motor car would help deliver unprecedented freedom and prosperity, was as much an illusion as the celluloid cities it was inspired by.

Coulter's Department Store, Los Angeles
Stiles O Clements, 1939

Eastern Columbia Building, Los Angeles
Claud Beelman, 1930

West Coast Radio City (NBC), Los Angeles
John C Austin, 1938

De La Warr Pavilion, Bexhill on Sea, East Sussex
Erich Mendelsohn and Serge Chermayeff, 1935

Streamline Moderne

For architects reluctant to pare their buildings down to Le Corbusier's vision of an architecture entirely stripped of applied decoration, the aesthetic of the ocean liner offered an alternative. Sleek, yet glamorous, the ever-increasing number of luxury cruise ships for the growing middle classes were the height of elegance. Many buildings adopted their curving forms, linear decoration, balcony rails and even sometimes, port-holes.

An alternative to this ocean-going chic emerged in Paris in 1925 where L'Exposition des Arts Decoratifs spawned its own distinctive and hugely influential style. The stepped blocks, stripes and coloured geometric detailing of Art Deco became the vogue, particularly for cinemas but also in industrial and commercial projects, and even housing.

Nineteen Eighteen-Four
George Orwell

A grim dystopia is overseen by party leader Big Brother. Winston Smith works for the Ministry of Truth, rewriting historical newspaper articles to reflect the current party line. Smith dreams of rebellion.

Nineteen-Eighty Four's themes include nationalism, censorship and surveillance. Orwell's searing critique of political power was set in a future Great Britain, a dictatorship at war. He imagined what totalitarian communism would be like if transported to English-speaking countries.

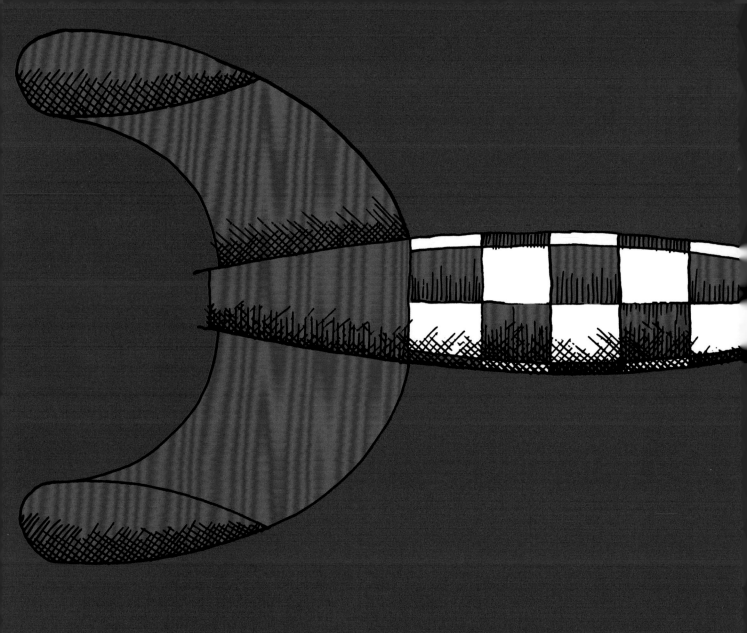

THE ERA OF THE ATOM

Optimism reigned in the years following the Second World War. Despite the unprecedented destructive threat of the atomic bomb and the political tensions arising from the division of Europe between democratic and communist states, the mood was forward-looking and positive. Average incomes rose steadily across Western Europe and the US, as did the aspirations of the growing middle class. On this happy tide a baby boom ensured, access to education improved and mass-production of motor cars, TVs and white goods changed patterns of life and leisure for millions.

The pace of technological change brought international travel within reach of ever-greater numbers. This was also the era of space exploration. The launch of the Russian *Sputnik 1* in October 1957 precipitated a space race that was a symptom of growing international tension. Lingering uncertainties after two world wars and regular sabre-rattling from the USSR and China played upon deep-rooted fears.

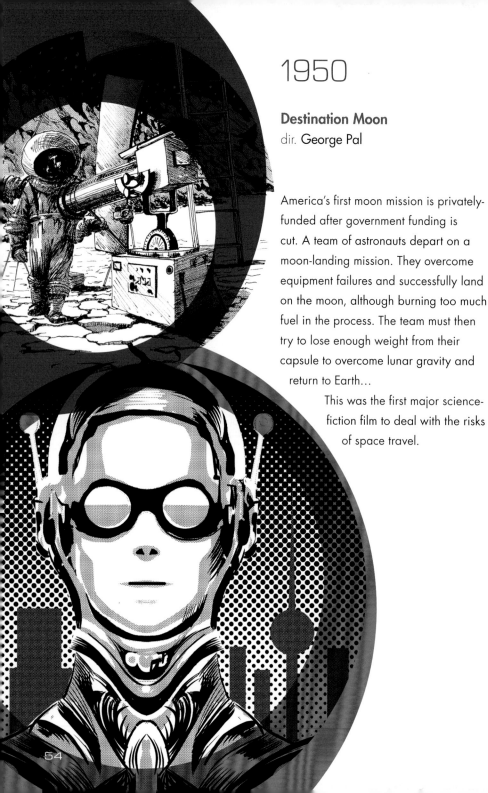

1950

Destination Moon
dir. George Pal

America's first moon mission is privately-funded after government funding is cut. A team of astronauts depart on a moon-landing mission. They overcome equipment failures and successfully land on the moon, although burning too much fuel in the process. The team must then try to lose enough weight from their capsule to overcome lunar gravity and return to Earth…

This was the first major science-fiction film to deal with the risks of space travel.

1950

I, Robot
Isaac Asimov

A collection of nine short stories, published in one volume. A linking narrative is provided by Dr Susan Calvin, a robopsychologist, reminiscing to a journalist about her life's work.

The stories introduce Asimov's Three Laws of Robotics, which have featured many times in popular culture. A 2004 film *I, Robot* (dir. Alex Proyas), starring Will Smith, is very loosely-based on one of the stories, *Little Lost Robot*, along with another Asimov novel, *The Caves of Steel*.

Dan Dare
Frank Hampson

The British equivalent of Buck Rogers, Dan Dare first appears in the *Eagle* comic. Chief pilot of the Interplanet Space Fleet, on a mission to Venus, he encounters the Mekon, despotic ruler of a futuristic city.

Drawn and scripted by Frank Hampson, the strip echoed the aspirations of Britain in the 1950s, recovering from war and looking towards a future transformed through technological prowess. Hampson pushed atomic-era design through the architecture of the strip's cityscapes, with London's skyline a vision of shard-like skyscrapers. London Transport monorail trains run through urban mountain ranges.

Dan Dare's influence on a generation of British architects growing up in the 1950s cannot be overstated. Norman Foster even commissioned a former *Eagle* artist to draw his Renault Distribution Centre in Swindon as a pull-out poster for the *Architectural Review* in 1983.

1951

The Day the Earth Stood Still
dir. Robert Wise

A spacecraft arrives on Earth and the alien Klaatu emerges, accompanied by powerful robot Gort. Klaatu's message is of crucial importance for the future of mankind.

The set designers collaborated with Frank Lloyd Wright on the design of the spacecraft. It has been suggested that the design was influenced by Wright's Johnson Wax Headquarters in Racine, Wisconsin, 1939. The story was based on the 1940 short story *Farewell to the Master* by Harry Bates, published in *Astounding Science Fiction*. It was remade in 2008 (dir. Scott Derrickson) starring Keanu Reaves.

1951

The Thing from Another World
dir. Christian Nyby

A humanoid body is discovered in a block of ice in the furthest reaches of the Arctic. When it is accidentally revived, the creature which emerges is intent on the destruction of humanity.

The film reflected a, post-Hiroshima, public view of scientists meddling with 'things better left alone'.

Remade in 1982 by John Carpenter as *The Thing*.

The Day of the Triffids
John Wyndham

Venomous carnivorous plants, capable
of movement and communication,
take over the world after most of the
population is blinded. Wyndham's
novel played upon fundamental human
fears and established him as one of the
leading exponents of the sci-fi genre.

The novel was made into a film in
1962 (dir. Steve Sekely), adapted for
radio and twice for television by the
BBC (in 1981 and 2009).

1953

The War of the Worlds
dir. Byron Haskin

A satirical commentary on the prevailing Cold War between the capitalist west and the communist east and the nuclear arms race. The film won an Academy Award for Best Visual Effects.

Steven Spielberg's 2005 version stars Tom Cruise.

1953

It Came from Outer Space
dir. Jack Arnold

A spaceship crashes in a mid-American town and the locals start to behave oddly. The aliens shape-shift into the appearance of people they kidnap to allow them to collect material to repair their ship.

The original story was by Ray Bradbury, and it was filmed in 3D, to add to the impact of this science-fiction horror story.

1953

Destination Moon
Hergé

In Syldavia, Professor Calculus is working on a top-secret project for a manned mission to the Moon. He invites Tintin and Captain Haddock to see his work.

Hergé extensively researched the possibility of space travel to try to make his comic books as realistic as possible. The design of the rocket is based on the German V-2, the world's first, long-range guided ballistic missile, developed during the Second World War. Even the decorative scheme on Tintin's rocket resembles the V-2.

Googie Architecture

Googie architecture was a spin-off from futurist architecture influenced by car culture, flight, the space race and the atomic age. Originating in Southern California during the late 1940s and extending to the mid 1960s, 'Googie' style was popular in the construction of motels, gas stations and diners. The name 'Googie' came from a coffee shop in West Hollywood, designed by the hugely innovative architect John Lautner in 1949.

Sweeping roofs, curved geometric shapes, starbursts and the bold use of glass, steel and neon pandered to the American fascination with the Space Age and the future. One of the most famous examples is the 'Welcome to Fabulous Las Vegas' sign.

The style later became known as part of the Mid-century modern school, an American reflection of the International Modern and Bauhaus movements, including the work of Walter Gropius, Le Corbusier and Mies van der Rohe.

Capitol Records Building, Los Angeles
Welton Becket, 1956

McDonald's Restaurant #3, Downey, California
Stanley Clark Meston, 1953

Schaffer Residence, Glendale, California
John Lautner, 1949

'Vandamm House' after Frank Lloyd Wright
MGM set designers created a studio set for *North by Northwest*
(dir. Alfred Hitchcock, 1959); the exteriors were matte paintings.

1954

Geodesic dome
R Buckminster Fuller

Although the first similar dome was designed in Germany after the First World War by Walther Bauersfeld for a planetarium, which opened to the public in 1926, it was Buckminster Fuller's lattice of interlocking icosahedrons which is credited with popularising the concept. He was awarded the US patent in 1954.

Geodesics ('great circles') on the dome or sphere intersect to form triangular (or hexagonal) elements, which are then simplified to provide as close to an exact sphere as can be achieved from flat, planar elements. A dome is extremely strong for its weight, encloses the greatest volume for the least surface area of any building and provides an inherently stable structure.

Soon after Fuller registered his patent and publicised the idea the geodesic dome started to be used for specialised construction projects, including auditoriums, weather observatories and storage facilities.

Fuller built his own personal dome home, the R Buckminster Fuller and Anne Hewlett Dome Home in Carbondale, Illinois in 1960, where he lived until 1971. Also in 1960, the Climatron greenhouse by TC Howard of Synergetics Inc opened in the Missouri Botanical Garden in St Louis.

Two pavilions at World's Fairs (New York, 1964 and Montreal, 1967) introduced the dome to a wider audience. Although the cover of the United States Pavilion from Expo 67 burned in the 1980s, the frame still exists and the structure now houses a museum dedicated to the environment.

Geodesic domes were also popularised by the movies, with the James Bond film *You Only Live Twice* (dir. Lewis Gilbert, 1967) featuring a dome in the opening sequence. *Silent Running* (dir. Douglas Trumbull, 1972) featured giant dome greenhouses on space freighters, bearing the last of Earth's plants. They remain a staple of science-fiction today, with recent examples featuring in *Doctor Who*'s *The Waters of Mars* (2009) and *X-Men: First Class* (dir. Matthew Vaughn, 2011).

The term 'Spaceship Earth' was coined by Fuller. The *Spaceship Earth* attraction at Walt Disney World Resort in Florida was designed with the help of Ray Bradbury, who also helped develop the storyline. The structure, a geodesic sphere, fifty metres in diameter, opened in 1982.

Geodesic domes are now regarded as icons of Cold War futurism with an air of Space Age efficiency. It is possible that, with interest in alternative housing on the increase, the geodesic dome may achieve renewed popularity.

Climatron, Missouri Botanical Garden
TC Howard, 1960

Geodesic domes from
You Only Live Twice
dir. Lewis Gilbert, 1967

American Pavilion (now Montreal Biosphère), Expo '67, Montreal
R Buckminster Fuller, 1967

Spacehip Earth, Walt Disney World Resort, Florida
Wallace Floyd Design Group, 1982

R Buckminster Fuller and Anne Hewlett Dome Home
Carbondale, Illinois
R Buckminster Fuller, 1960

65

Explorers on the Moon
Hergé

Them!
dir. Gordon Douglas

Tintin, Snowy, Captain Haddock and Professor Calculus head towards the Moon in an atomic-powered spaceship. Unfortunately bumbling detectives Thomson and Thompson have stowed away on board. The oxygen supply is not sufficient to keep them all alive…

In this early 'nuclear monster' film a nest of gigantic ants is discovered in the desert of New Mexico. A queen sets out to establish a new nest and the United States is under threat…

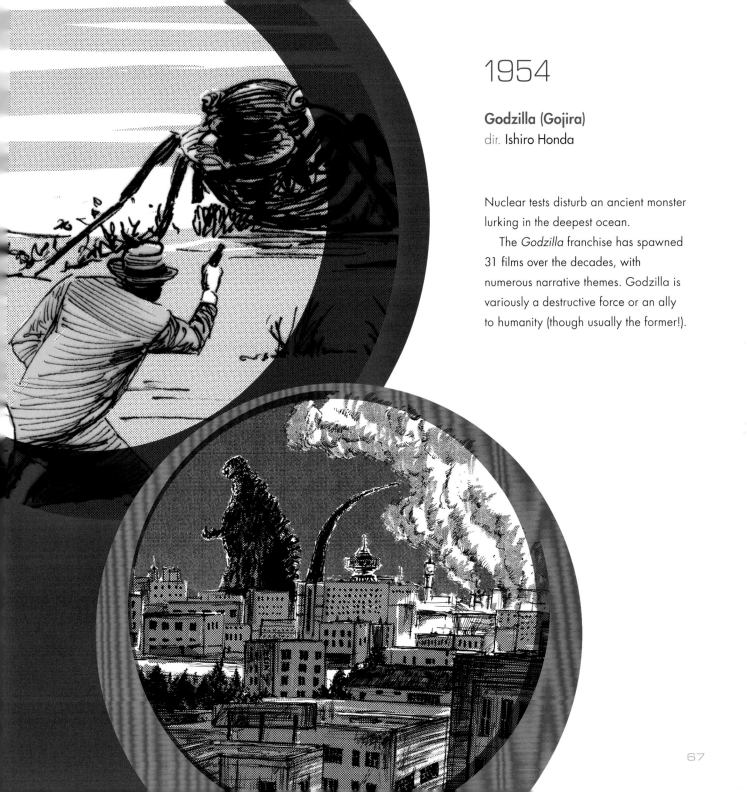

1954

Godzilla (Gojira)
dir. Ishiro Honda

Nuclear tests disturb an ancient monster lurking in the deepest ocean.

The *Godzilla* franchise has spawned 31 films over the decades, with numerous narrative themes. Godzilla is variously a destructive force or an ally to humanity (though usually the former!).

1955

Invasion of the Body Snatchers
dir. Don Siegel

A Californian town is scattered by
seeds which fall from outer space
and grow into large pods. The pods
generate copies of people near them.
The duplicates are without human
emotion. A local doctor discovers
what is happening and tries to stop
the process. The fear of communist
invasion had already prompted
Senator McCarthy to start his
crack-down on infiltration – this
film comments of these themes.

1956

1984
dir. Michael Anderson

George Orwell's hero, Winston Smith, an 'everyman' character accused of
subversion is, ultimately, broken by the system. The urban scenes depict a
menacing, relentless modernism, repetitive and joyless. Giant screens relay the
dictat of 'Big Brother'. This first film version of Orwell's masterpiece exploits post-
Nazi fears of totalitarianism.

Michael Radford directed a version of the film released in 1984, starring John
Hurt, Richard Burton and Suzanna Hamilton, with a soundtrack by Eurythmics.

1956

Forbidden Planet
dir. Fred Wilcox

With a narrative loosely-based on Shakespeare's *The Tempest*, *Forbidden Planet* was the first science-fiction film set entirely away from Earth. It featured the first filmic depiction of humans travelling in their own, faster-than-light, spacecraft. A crew is dispatched from Earth to discover the fate of a lost expedition from twenty years earlier. Upon arrival on a planet they discover a fantastic, abandoned alien underground city and meet the mysterious Dr Morbius and his daughter Altaira.

Robbie the Robot is one of the first robots in film to have a personality and be a significant character in the narrative in his own right.

The ambitious sets included the 'great machine', an archetype for immense, interior architectural structures in science-fiction film.

Mid-century Modern

By the middle of the twentieth century, the modern movement in architecture was the predominant style for cultural monuments and most civic and commercial architecture. Techniques and components had become increasingly sophisticated and customised materials and solutions were adopted to address most aspects of the complex delivery of buildings.

As with all architectural approaches, a number of individuals emerged who, in their home nations, and increasingly internationally were recognised as modernist masters. The Brazilian Oscar Niemeyer (1907-2012) worked directly with Le Corbusier on the United Nations HQ in New York. The Finnish architect, Alvar Aalto (1898-1976) evolved his own style from a strict linear approach to something more organic.

Brutalism

The word 'Brutalism' is sometimes used, pejoratively, as a synonym for 'brutal' when describing buildings the viewer dislikes. However, the architectural application actually originates in the term Le Corbusier used to describe a favourite material, 'béton brut' (raw concrete).

Brutalism flourished from the 1950s to the 1970s. Massy, sculptural, exposed concrete structures were created for, in the main, civic or institutional clients. Their chunky, often fortress-like, character was perhaps a modernist expression of gravitas, reliability, corporate responsibility. The style was popular with universities and, perhaps less predictably, applied to some high-rise housing and even shopping centres.

Habitat 67, 1967 World's Fair, Montreal
Moshe Safdie, 1967

Cité Radieuse, Marseille
Le Corbusier, 1952

Nuffield Transplantation Surgery Unit, Edinburgh
Peter Womersley, 1968

1959

The Twilight Zone
CBS

Under the guise of a title redolent of mystery, this TV series, by Rod Sterling, explored horror, psychological thriller and fantasy themes as well as science-fiction. In an era when many political subjects were off-limits it was possible to explore such topics under the guise of these darkly themed adventures. Senator McCarthy, whose witch-hunt against communist infiltrators within the movie industry and the media was in full swing, may not have spotted the subterfuge.

The Twilight Zone's commercial and critical success led to numerous spin-offs spanning five decades, including two further TV series.

1960

Village of the Damned
dir. Wolf Rilla

This British film version of the classic 1957 novel *The Midwich Cuckoos* faithfully follows John Wyndham's original narrative. After all the inhabitants of an English village are temporarily struck unconscious, the women are found to be pregnant. After they give birth on the same day their children develop at an unnatural pace and share telepathic powers.

MGM shelved the original, American production, begun in 1957, after bowing to pressure from religious groups objecting to the 'miraculous' births.

The Day the Earth Caught Fire
dir. Val Guest

The United States and USSR carry out simultaneous nuclear tests and a journalist discovers a rapid rise in global temperatures. The solution is further nuclear detonations intended to move the Earth away from the Sun and return it to its usual orbit.

Partly-filmed on location in London and Brighton, matte paintings depicted abandoned cities and desolate landscapes.

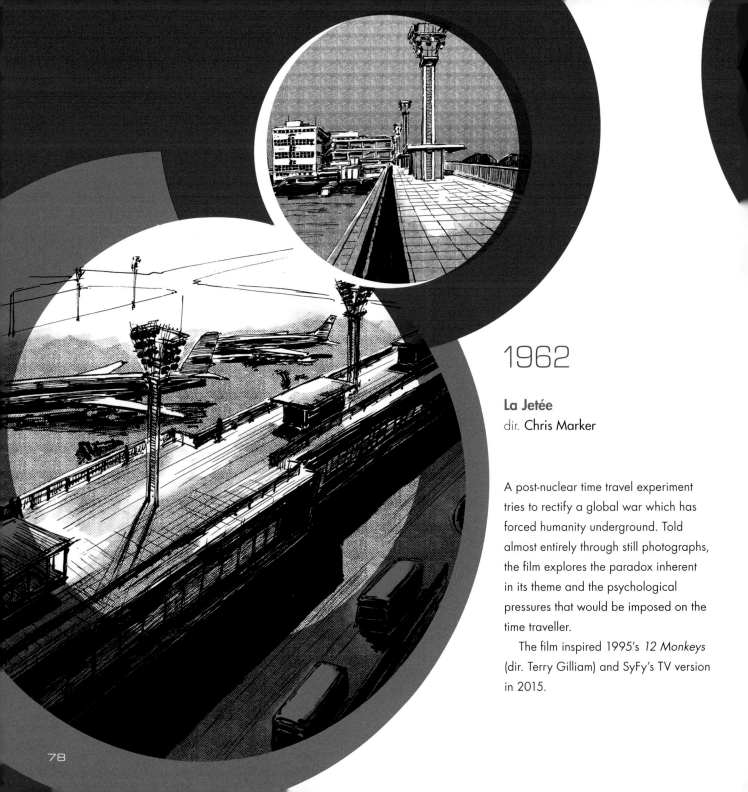

1962

La Jetée
dir. **Chris Marker**

A post-nuclear time travel experiment tries to rectify a global war which has forced humanity underground. Told almost entirely through still photographs, the film explores the paradox inherent in its theme and the psychological pressures that would be imposed on the time traveller.

The film inspired 1995's *12 Monkeys* (dir. Terry Gilliam) and SyFy's TV version in 2015.

1963

Doctor Who
BBC

First broadcast by the BBC
on 23 November 1963, with
William Hartnell as The Doctor, a
mysterious figure travelling through
space and time in his, bigger-on-
the-inside, TARDIS, the outer shell of
which has become 'stuck' in the form of
a London police box. The second story,
The Mutants, saw the advent of the
Daleks, created by Terry Nation.

The concept of regeneration was
introduced by the production team to
address Hartnell's failing health, thus
allowing the lead role to be re-cast
and the show to continue. Seven actors
played the Time Lord until the series was
cancelled in 1989.

1965

Alphaville
dir. Jean-Luc Goddard

In the technocratic dictatorship of the city of Alphaville, the evil Dr von Braun is responsible for Alpha 60, a computer which oppressively controls the city. Poetry and emotion are outlawed. The computer is finally defeated by intergalactic agent Lemmy Caution, who provides poetic answers to its questioning.

The modernist, glass and concrete buildings of 1960s Paris became the set for this dystopian film noir. No special sets or props were used.

1966

Fahrenheit 451
dir. François Truffaut

In a totalitarian future, all literature is banned. In his 1953 novel Ray Bradbury proposed 451°F as the auto-ignition point of paper. A fireman, whose duty is to burn all literature, becomes a fugitive for the crime of reading.

Truffaut's only film in English was also his first in colour. Partially shot at the renowned Brutalist and Scandinavian Modernist inspired Alton Estate, Roehampton, London, by a London County Council team, led by Rosemary Stjernstedt.

The monorail scene was filmed at French consortium SAFEGE's suspended test track at Châteauneuf-sur-Loire.

1966

Star Trek
NBC

Gene Roddenberry's *Star Trek* was first broadcast on the US network NBC. William Shatner takes the captain's chair in the first adventures of the USS *Enterprise* NCC-1701.

Star Trek was one of the first sci-fi series to commission scripts from contemporary novelists, including Robert Bloch and Harlan Ellison. Dorothy C Fontana, script editor and author of several episodes, was encouraged by Roddenberry to use her initials as he felt that a woman might not be taken seriously in a male-dominated field.

The series often used its future setting to comment on social issues of the 1960s, including sexism, racism, religion, narrow notions of nationalism and nuclear brinkmanship.

Although cancelled after three seasons, it was later a hit in syndication, achieving cult status. *Star Trek* is now widely considered one of the most influential television series of all time.

1968

Planet of the Apes
dir. Franklin J Schaffner

This film is based on the 1963 novel by French author Pierre Boulle (who also wrote *Bridge Over the River Kwai*), with a script written by Rod Sterling. The crew of a space craft, including Charlton Heston's character, George Taylor, crash-land on a mysterious planet far into the future. In a strange inversion, the planet is dominated by highly intelligent apes. The final scene is one of the most iconic in the history of cinema.

Four sequels and a television series followed in the 1970s, with a 're-imagining' of the first film in 2001 (dir. Tim Burton), which received mixed reviews.

A new rebooted film series opened with *Rise of the Planet of the Apes* in 2011 (dir. Rupert Wyatt) followed by 2014's *Dawn of the Planet of the Apes* (dir. Matt Reeves). *War for the Planet of the Apes* will appear in cinemas in 2017 also directed by Matt Reeves.

"Stanley Kubrick made the ultimate science-fiction movie, and it is going to be very hard for someone to come along and make a better movie, as far as I'm concerned. On a technical level, it can be compared, but personally I think that '2001' is far superior."

George Lucas
1977

1968

2001: A Space Odyssey
dir. **Stanley Kubrick**

Partially-based on the novella *The Sentinel of Eternity* by Arthur C Clarke (written in 1948 and submitted as an entry in a BBC competition, subsequently published in *Ten Story Fantasy* in 1951), the screenplay was co-written by the director and Clarke.

Astronauts travel to Jupiter onboard *Discovery One* with the sentient computer Hal 9000, after the discovery of a mysterious black monolith which has been affecting human evolution. Themes included artificial intelligence, alien life and existentialism.

The impressive, detailed sets featured furniture and props by modern designers including cutlery by Arne Jacobsen, desks by Herman Miller, pedestal tables by Eero Saarinen and bright red Djinn chairs by Oliver Mourgue. Even the typography was carefully selected, with the modernist typefaces Eurostile Bold Extended and Futura used extensively.

Stylish, cool, awash with special effects, scientifically accurate and accompanied by a highly memorable soundtrack, it is little wonder that *2001* is a classic.

THE EDGE OF DESTRUCTION

After years of the bright optimism despite the very real threats of the Atomic Age, film-makers, in part influenced by the New Wave authors of the 1960s (including Brian Aldiss, JG Ballard, William Burroughs, Harlan Ellison, Ursula Le Guin, Michael Moorcock and Robert Silverberg), turned to dark distortions in their depictions of possible futures. This new style of science-fiction was less concerned with scientific credibility than the literary qualities of the work.

In many films of this era the masses are downtrodden under the grip of evil galactic empires. Encounters with aliens become terrifying. Futuristic cities are places where cut-throat corporations rule and the Earth is frequently on the verge of cataclysm.

Science-fiction paralleled contemporary issues of environmental change and concerns over energy waste. Buckminster Fuller's 1961 image of Manhattan under a giant dome was used in a 1971 poster, urging 'Save Our Planet!'.

1970

THX 1138
dir. George Lucas

In a bleak, dystopian future the populace is controlled using emotion-suppressing drugs. Android police officers punish any infractions.

George Lucas' directorial debut was filmed in and around San Francisco. Among the film's locations were the Bay Area Rapid Transit subway (BART) and Frank Lloyd Wright's futuristic Marin County Civic Centre (1960).

Not commercially successful on release, the film has gone on to have a cult following, particularly after the success of Lucas' *Star Wars* in 1977.

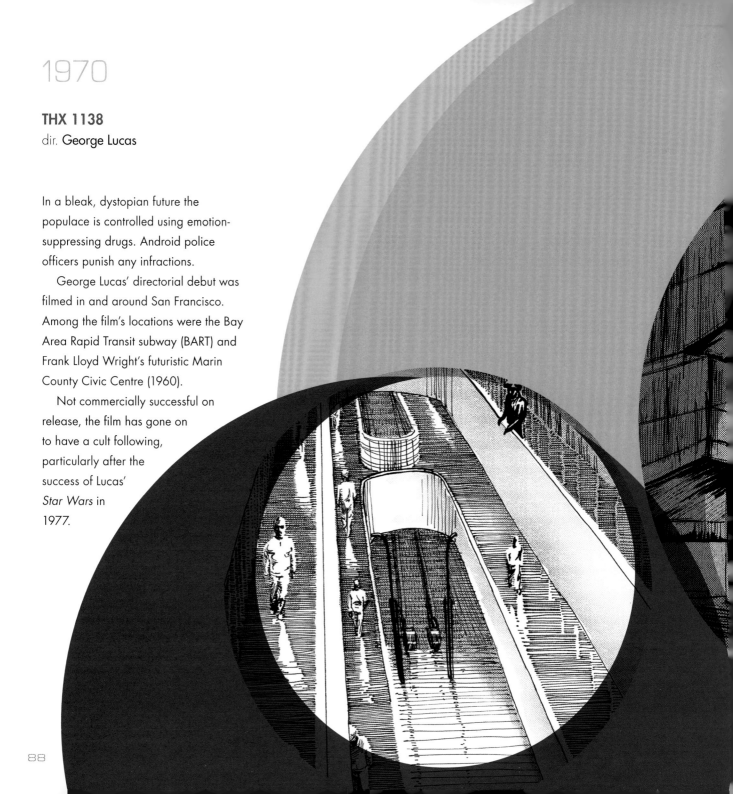

1971

A Clockwork Orange
dir. **Stanley Kubrick**

Based on the 1962 novel by Anthony Burgess, *A Clockwork Orange* depicts a violent near-future Britain, where ordinary citizens live in a state of fear, constantly under threat.

It was filmed mainly on location around London, including in Garnett Cloughley Blakemore & Associates' Chelsea Drugstore of 1968 and at the modernist Thamesmead Housing Estate, constructed in the late 1960s. Its design included elevated walkways and water as a 'calming influence' on the residents.

As well as A Clockwork Orange, Thamesmead features prominently in Channel 4's *Beautiful Thing* (dir. Hettie MacDonald, 1996) and E4's *Misfits*, a science-fiction comedy drama, created by Howard Overman (2009-2013).

Hettie MacDonald also directed the, Hugo Award-winning, *Blink* episode of *Doctor Who* in 2007.

1972

Silent Running
dir. **Douglas Trumbull**

The last few plants are tended in enormous geodesic domes on space freighters. Bruce Dern stars as Freeman Lowell, a botanist and ecologist, one of four crewmen. He spends most of his time tending the plants in the dome, with the help of service robots Huey, Dewey and Louie (in homage to Donald Duck's nephews).

The domes of the space freighters were based on the, Buckminster Fuller inspired, Climatron geodesic dome at the Missouri Botanical Garden.

Trumbull had previously worked as special effects supervisor on *2001: A Space Odyssey* and 1971's *The Andromeda Strain* (dir. Robert Wise).

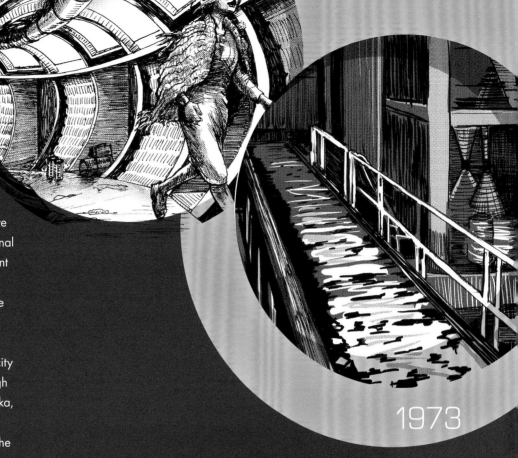

1972

Solaris
dir. Andrei Tarkovsky

In this Soviet adaptation of Stanisław Lem's 1961 novel, the crew of three scientists aboard a space station have fallen into separate emotional crises. A psychologist is sent to Solaris station, only to encounter the same strange phonomena affecting the crew.

The scenes of the future city that a space pilot flies through in the film were shot in Akasaka, Toyko in 1971, after delays caused an earlier plan to shoot the futuristic structures at Expo '70 in Osaka to fall through.

Steven Soderbergh directed a remake of Solaris in 2002, starring George Clooney and Natascha McElhone.

1973

Soylent Green
dir. Richard Fleischer

The plot, loosely based on Harry Harrison's novel *Make Room! Make Room!* (1968) sees Charlton Heston playing a police detective investigating the murder of a businessman. The setting is a future Earth where the greenhouse effect has raised temperatures, resources are depleted and the world is massively overpopulated. Lack of food is a real issue and international leaders agree to supplying the mysterious Soylent Green, artificial nourishment whose manufacturer is shrouded in secrecy, as the solution.

1973

Sleeper
dir. Woody Allen

Woody Allen plays a cryogenically frozen health shop owner who is awakened after 200 years into a disorganised police state.

One prominent location used in the film was 1963's Sculptured House in Genesee Mountain, Colorado by Charles Deaton. The sweeping concrete curves and white-moulded forms suggest streamlined and integrated services and advanced materials.

Space: 1999
ITV

The moon is hurled out of Earth's orbit after explosions in atomic-waste dumps. Moonbase Alpha's inhabitants seek a new home amongst the stars.

Created by Gerry and Sylvia Anderson, *Space: 1999* was, at the time, the most expensive series on British television. It drew visual inspiration and technical expertise from *2001: A Space Odyssey*. The 'Moon City' uniforms were created by Austrian fashion designer Rudi Gernreich. Sets were dressed with contemporary furnishings, including lamps by Guzzini and Gae Aulenti and chairs by Vico Magistretti.

American stars Martin Landau and Barbara Bain led the cast. Special effects director Brian Johnson and his team went on to work on 1979's *Alien* (dir. Ridley Scott) and 1980's *The Empire Strikes Back* (dir. Irvin Kershner).

1974

Dark Star
dir. John Carpenter

This black comedy spoof-take on *2001* was described in its posters and promotion as a "Spaced Out Odyssey".

The poster for the film featured the tagline 'The Spaced Out Odyssey'. The scout ship *Dark Star* is on a mission to destroy 'unstable planets' and uses artificial intelligence to pursue this goal. The 'rushing stars' effect depicting faster-than-light space travel, taken up later by *Star Trek* and *Star Wars*, was first used in this film.

1976

Logan's Run
dir. Michael Anderson

In a future society, in the City of Domes, Logan 5 (Michael York), a 'sandman', runs with Jessica 6 (Jenny Aguter) from the state-sanctioned requirement that he die at thirty.

On the surface the city is a hedonistic utopia, covered by geodesic domes. The service tunnels underneath the shining buildings are industrial, grim and neglected. Once outside the domes, seeking 'Sanctuary', they discover the remains of Washington which have been overrun by nature.

The film was among the first to use lasers and holograms in its special effects.

1977

Star Wars
dir. **George Lucas**

A long time ago, in a galaxy far, far, away, a group of rebels attempt to overthrow a totalitarian empire. And thus was born the highest-grossing film franchise of all time. In the first film a group of attractive and energetic young people, including the relatively unknown Harrison Ford, are pitted against the dark forces of evil, personified by the, black-clad, Darth Vader.

Light relief is provided by Ford's character's personal dilemma, whether to 'do the right thing' or stick to his established mercenary habits, by the love interest of a royalty/commoner forbidden relationship and by the robot pairing of the whistling R2D2 with the campest humanoid in film history.

While much of the action takes place aboard various starships, the architecture of the garrison spaceship, Death Star in the spectacular climax is an extruded, endless dense mountainscape of stacked, soulless blocks, one of the bleakest visions of the distorted city in all cinema.

Designed by the English one-time architectural model-maker and former James Bond set designer John Stears, the Death Star was conceived as a spherical spaceship of planetary scale – city become weapon of mass destruction.

Two sequels and three prequels followed, and a new trilogy, set thirty years after the events of *Return of the Jedi*, began with *The Force Awakens* in 2015 (dir JJ Abrams).

Capricorn One
dir. **Peter Hyams**

Journalist Robert Caulfield (Elliot Gould) investigates a government conspiracy surrounding a Mars landing hoax.

Peter Hyams conceived the concept after working on the Apollo mission broadcasts. No doubt the Watergate scandal, leading to the resignation of President Nixon on 9 August 1974, also played a part. Lew Grade's production company ITC, which had also produced shows including *The Prisoner*, *Thunderbirds*, *Space: 1999* and *The Muppet Show*, provided the budget. Despite the not entirely complimentary portrayal of the agency, NASA supplied props.

Close Encounters of the Third Kind
dir. **Steven Spielberg**

The life of Roy Neary (Richard Dreyfuss) changes after an encounter with an unidentified flying object. He is drawn, with others, to the Devil's Tower in Wyoming, a mountain that rises dramatically from the plains below. A gigantic mothership descends as scientists try to communicate with the aliens using sound and light.

Douglas Trumbull supervised the visual effects; he joked that with a budget of $3.3m he could have produced an additional film. The design of the mothership, by Ralph McQuarrie, was inspired by Spielberg's sight of an Indian oil refinery at night.

1977

2000AD / Judge Dredd

First published on 26 February 1977 by IPC Magazines, *2000AD* is a British weekly science-fiction based comic. Most famous for its *Judge Dredd* stories, contributors have included Alan Moore, Neil Gaiman, Grant Morrison, Brian Bolland, Mike McMahon and Jamie Hewlett. Many contributors have gone on to work for American publishers including DC Comics and Marvel Comics.

Judge Dredd is a law-enforcement officer in Mega-City One, set in North America. He is a 'street judge', who can arrest, convict, sentence and execute criminals. Created by writer John Wagner, editor Pat Mills and artist Carlos Ezquerra, the setting of Judge Dredd is a dystopian future Earth devastated by war, with most of the planet a radioactive wasteland. The population, mostly unemployed due to automation, live in gigantic towers in the city which has developed from the sprawl of America's east coast.

1978

Blake's 7
BBC

Created by Terry Nation, this story of renegades fighting a totalitarian Earth Federation, ran for four series. The populace are observed through mass surveillence, kept passive by mood-altering drugs, and dissidents are brainwashed or harshly punished. On Earth, citizens live in a giant 'arcology' (a sustainable human environment, providing for all human needs – habitation, work and leisure, within one mega building – the term conflates 'architecture' and 'ecology') in the shape of a dome. On the outer planets, the people struggle to survive.

Authoritarian dystopias were a common theme in Nation's work, the most famous being the Nazi-inspired origin story for the Daleks, in 1975's *Genesis of the Daleks* story in *Doctor Who*, which introduced Davros, the creator of the Daleks.

The Hitchhiker's Guide to the Galaxy
Douglas Adams

Adam's seminal sci-fi comedy, was first broadcast on BBC Radio 4. Hapless Arthur Dent hitchhikes on a spacecraft with alien Ford Prefect after the Earth is demolished to make way for a new hyperspace bypass.

Hugely popular, the series spawned five books, a TV series, two albums and a towel. A film was released in 2005 (dir. Garth Jennings) with Martin Freeman as the world-weary, dressing-gown wearing, Arthur Dent and Stephen Fry narrating as the voice of 'the guide' (not quite achieving the laconic delivery of Peter Jones who played 'the book' in the original radio series).

In the film, the Vogsphere is the home planet of the most pedantic, unpleasant bureaucrats in the universe. The Vogon city is a relentless mass of towering, uniform, rectangular grey concrete blocks representing the utter pointless tediousness of the inhabitants' lives.

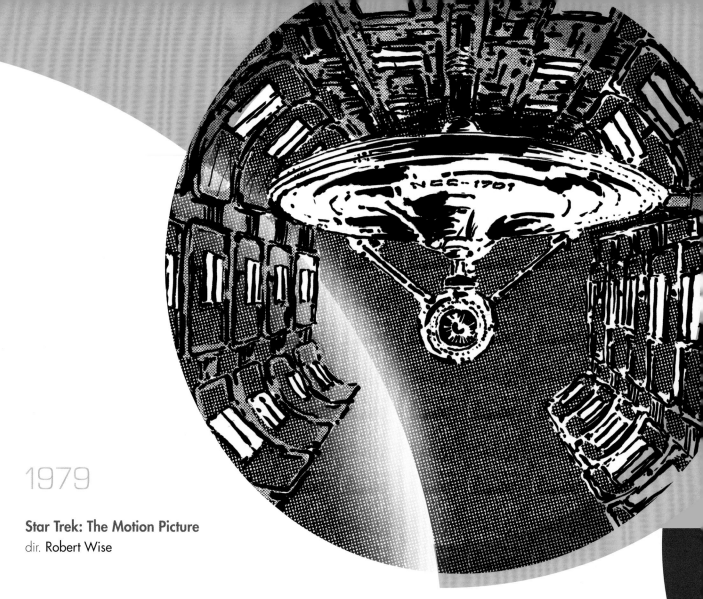

1979

Star Trek: The Motion Picture
dir. Robert Wise

A massive cloud of energy is moving through space towards Earth, destroying everything in its path. The newly-refitted *Enterprise* is the only ship in its way…

Although a script was developed for a *Star Trek* film in 1975, Paramount wasn't happy with it and decided to develop a new TV series, *Star Trek: Phase II*. After the success of *Star Wars* and *Close Encounters of the Third Kind*, the studio cancelled *Phase II* and the series' pilot, *In Thy Image*, was rapidly redeveloped into a film script.

The film wasn't well received but made enough at the box office for a cheaper sequel, 1982's *The Wrath of Khan*. Four further sequels followed featuring the crew from the original series.

1979

Alien
dir. Ridley Scott

A highly-aggressive extraterrestrial creature stalks and kills the crew of the spaceship *Nostromo*.

With inspiration from other science-fiction and horror films, including *The Thing from Another World* and *Forbidden Planet*, Dan O'Bannon's screenplay for *Alien* was highly influential. The horrific, biomechanical alien and its environment, by Swiss artist HR Giger, are a seminal design.

Three further films followed, *Aliens* in 1986 (dir. James Cameron), *Alien³* in 1992 (dir. David Fincher) and 1997's *Alien Resurrection* (dir. Jean-Pierre Jeunet). Ridley Scott returned to the franchise with prequel *Prometheus* in 2012 and *Alien: Covenant*, to be released in 2017. The lead character, Ellen Ripley, played by Sigourney Weaver in all four main series films, is credited as one of the most significant female protagonists in all cinema.

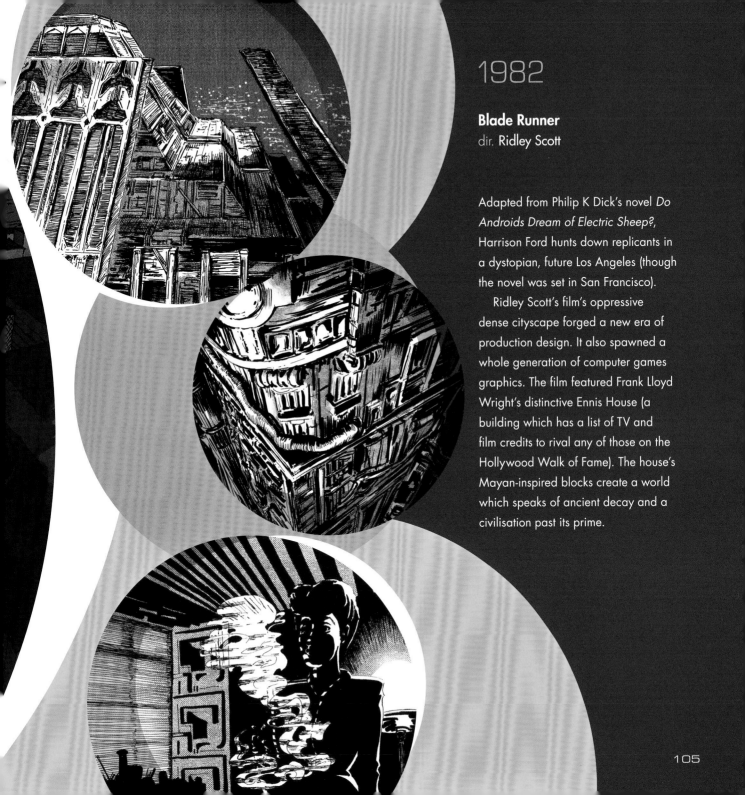

1982

Blade Runner
dir. Ridley Scott

Adapted from Philip K Dick's novel *Do Androids Dream of Electric Sheep?*, Harrison Ford hunts down replicants in a dystopian, future Los Angeles (though the novel was set in San Francisco).

Ridley Scott's film's oppressive dense cityscape forged a new era of production design. It also spawned a whole generation of computer games graphics. The film featured Frank Lloyd Wright's distinctive Ennis House (a building which has a list of TV and film credits to rival any of those on the Hollywood Walk of Fame). The house's Mayan-inspired blocks create a world which speaks of ancient decay and a civilisation past its prime.

1982

E.T. The Extra-Terrestrial
dir. **Steven Spielberg**

A lonely young boy befriends a stranded alien and tries to help it return home, whilst attempting to keep it hidden, both from his mother and the government. Spielberg's tale, partly based on his own childhood imaginary friend, was the highest grossing film of the 1980s. Its success was perhaps less about its science fiction genre than its universal themes of alienation, family, identity, friendship and loyalty.

Combining elements of comedy, narrative tension and pathos in almost equal measure, the story is played out against dull, slightly run-down, suburbia, a familiar banal everywhere.

1982

Tron
dir. **Steven Lisberger**

A computer programmer (Jeff Bridges) is transported inside the software world of a mainframe computer. Produced by Walt Disney Productions and combining live-action with back-lit and computer animation, the film was groundbreaking. Freed from the constraints of any simulation of the physical world the film's 'architecture' drew upon the linear renderings of 3D space from contemporary computer gaming.

Although not a great box office success, *Tron* built a cult following, in part perhaps because of nostalgic affection for early games. *Tron Legacy* (dir. Joesph Kasinski) reprised Jeff Bridges' role in 2010.

1984

Brazil
dir. Terry Gilliam

Brazil satirises industrial society. The action is played out within a bureaucratic, totalitarian, dystopian society, over-reliant on poorly maintained machines.

Gilliam commented that his film was "the Nineteen Eighty-Four for 1984." His films are renowned for their meticulous lighting and Brazil, set in an indeterminate future, rich in reference to cinema history, is a visual feast. He described the architecture of the movie as being neither past nor future and commented that it could be, "Belgrade or Scunthorpe on a drizzly day in February".

1984

The Terminator
dir. James Cameron

Filmed in Los Angeles with the city at night as the backdrop to much of the action, a killing machine is sent from the future to destroy man's best hope for survival.

Arnold Schwarzenegger plays the robot assassin which arrives from 2029 in order to kill the mother of the, yet to be born, John Connor, who is destined to save humanity from machine domination in a post-apocalyptic future. The film was a hit at the box office and spawned four sequels, comic books and video games.

Neuromancer
William Gibson

A washed-up computer hacker is hired by a mysterious employer to pull off the ultimate hack. Considered the archetypal cyberpunk novel, *Neuromancer* was the first of Gibson's Sprawl trilogy, followed by *Count Zero* and *Mona Lisa Overdrive*.

"High overhead, in the reflected glare of arc lamps, one of the unfinished Fuller domes shut out two thirds of the salmon-pink evening sky, its ragged edge like broken gray honeycomb. The Sprawl's patchwork of domes tended to generate inadvertent microclimates; there were areas of a few city blocks where a fine drizzle of condensation fell continually from the soot-stained geodesics, and sections of high dome famous for displays of static-discharge, a peculiarly urban variety of lightning."

William Gibson
Neuromancer

1987

Star Trek: The Next Generation
Paramount Domestic Television

A new series of Star Trek beamed onto
TV. Patrick Stewart led as Captain
Jean-Luc Picard on the Galaxy-class
USS *Enterprise* NCC-1701-D. Over the
next seven years a total of 178 episodes
were filmed. The new series is set about
70 years after the last voyage of the
original *Enterprise* Crew.

At $1.3 million an episode the new
series was one of the most expensive
one-hour TV dramas of its
era. The series led to *Deep
Space Nine*, *Voyager* and
Enterprise.

1987

RoboCop
dir. **Paul Verhoeven**

This cyberpunk action film is set in a crime-ridden Detroit of the near future. A police officer murdered by a criminal gang is revived as a superhuman cyborg law enforcer.

Much of the film was shot, not in Detroit but in Dallas, Texas where the Reunion Tower (Welton Becket & Associates, 1978) and other futuristic structures helped place the action firmly in an era yet to come. The 1986 Ford Taurus (Ford Scorpio in the UK) which played the patrol car was also considered the shape of things to come.

1988

Akira
dir. **Katsuhiro Otomo**

Considered a landmark in Japanese animation (anime), this film depicts a dystopian version of Toyko in the year 2019. Teenage biker Tetsuo attempts to release an imprisoned psychic, Akira.

Based on the cyberpunk manga comic book series serialised between 1982 and 1990, the film broke new ground in anime by its detailed depiction of the future city of Neo-Tokyo and detailed animation. The film has been cited as a major influence on films including *The Matrix* (dir. The Wachowskis).

THE TRIP OF A LIFETIME

After the end of the cold war, popular science-fiction gradually becomes more hopeful, whilst looking at themes including the expanding information universe with the rise of the internet and artificial intelligence, bio- and nanotechnology, post-scarcity societies and environmental activism.

Television and Hollywood look to the past for inspiration, with a number of films and shows being re-imagined or sequels created, all with new, state-of-the-art, computer-generated effects.

The resurgence of 'young adult' literature (almost single-handedly revived by the success of JK Rowling's *Harry Potter* series) produces new dystopian futures with teenage protagonists, principal among them Suzanne Collins' *The Hunger Games* and Veronica Roth's *Divergent*.

1990

Total Recall
dir. **Paul Verhoeven**

Its plot based on Philip K Dick's 1966 short story *We Can Remember It for You Wholesale*, Douglas Quaid (Arnold Schwarzenegger) is a construction worker having troubling dreams of Mars.

Mexico City's subway system and vehicles stood in for the futuristic subway station featured in the film. Schwarzenegger controlled virtually every aspect of the production of the film, which was one of the most expensive of the time. Fortunately for Arnold, it made its money back, and much more, at the box office.

A new version starring Colin Farrell was released in 2012 (dir. Len Wiseman) to poor reviews.

1991

Terminator 2: Judgement Day
dir. **James Cameron**

Breakthroughs in computer-generated effects, including the first use of natural human motion for a computer generated character were among the innovations to feature in this second outing of the *Terminator* series which trumped *Total Recall* as the most expensive film ever made. Both the director and the film's star had risen in stature since the first outing of the franchise.

Schwarzenegger's Terminator is benign this time (at least to the John Connor character). Once again, good triumphs – but the future, foretold in the narrative, is dark and uncertain.

1993

Jurassic Park
dir. **Steven Spielberg**

Based on the 1990 novel by Michael Crichton. This story of a doomed theme park, where dinosaurs are the star attraction, takes further giant leaps in the advancement of special effects. The park itself, with its massive, buttressed concrete structures, is designed to provide reassurance. The high fences surrounding the dinosaur enclosures are set in firm concrete foundations.

The film's production designer, Rick Carter, drew upon fantasy films and the architecture of John Lautner with twists all of his own including historic South American references and grass roofs – generating a sort of Mayan Moderne.

1993

The X-Files
Fox

Created by Chris Carter, this cult series followed FBI agents Fox Mulder (David Duchovny) and Dana Scully (Gillian Anderson) solving unexplained and paranormal cases. It played to the 1990s preoccupations with conspiracy theories and spirituality.

It ran for ten series, up to 2002. Although alien themes are at its core, *The X-Files* is pretty cross-genre, with horror, mystery and detective fiction as its inspiration. Mulder and Scully were reunited in a revival in 2016.

1996

Independence Day
dir. Roland Emmerich

1997

Stargate SG-1
Showtime

A modern take on *The War of the Worlds*. Aliens invade the world in gigantic ships, but are defeated with the help of a virus, in this case a computer virus sent from Jeff Goldblum's Apple Macintosh Powerbook 5300. Not unlike the Death Star in *Star Wars*, the immense mothership is a great garrison city in space. As the Goldblum character and his sidekick, played by Will Smith, travel towards its core (in an alien attack ship which had crash-landed in Roswell in 1947) they fly through giant, angled, tower structures with bulbous, organic extrusions and lit windows – hinting at the beings who dwell within.

Inspired by the 1994 film, a military team defend Earth from alien threats by travelling to distant planets via a wormhole. The series ran for ten years and two films, making it the longest-running sci-fi show on US television. *Stargate Atlantis* and *Stargate Universe* followed.

1997

The Fifth Element
dir. Luc Besson

In this English-language, French, science-fiction actioner, Bruce Willis must help Milla Jovovich recover four mystical stones to defend Earth against an impending attack.

The production design was by comic book illustrators – which contributes to the bright, colour-clashing, imagery of the movie. Besson declared that he was tired of the dark landscapes of many science fiction films and wanted something "cheerfully crazy" instead.

Much of the action takes place in a reinvented New York, combining modular apartment blocks from the 1960s with Art Deco detailing and Futurist imagery from Sant'Elia in the 1910s.

To achieve the effects Besson wanted, dozens of apartment buildings and 25 skyscrapers were meticulously modelled

at 1/24th scale – complete with interior décor – only glimpsed in fly-post shots. Further crazy cheerfulness was contributed by Jean-Paul Gaultier, whose gender-bending costume designs were, like the movie itself, among the most expensive in European cinema history.

119

Blob Architecture

'Blobitecture' has its origins in the highly influential theories of the early 1960s Archigram group based at London's Architectural Association (AA) whose leaders included the architects Peter Cook (now Sir Peter) and Ron Herron. Their ideas, expounded in their pamphlet *Archigram I* (1961) explored modular living and their visionary images of fantastical, technological structures were widely published.

The May 1964 'Zoom' issue of the *Archigram* magazine drew its inspiration from popular science-fiction comic book imagery. Through their influence, their teaching and the increasing structural complexity enabled by computerised structural analysis, a number of buildings which relate directly to their ideas and theories have emerged in recent years.

A number of AA graduates, notably Dame Zaha Hadid (1950-2016) and Kathryn Findlay (1953-2014) as well as Peter Cook himself have created important curvilinear works quite at odds with the orthodoxy of the orthogonal.

Guggenheim Museum, Bilbao
Frank Gehry, 1997

**Kunsthaus Graz
(Graz Art Museum)
Graz, Austria**
Peter Cook and Colin Fournier, 2003

Selfridges, Birmingham
Future Systems, 2003

Sage Gateshead
Foster and Partners, 2004

Riverside Museum, Glasgow
Zaha Hadid Architects, 2011

Gattaca
dir. Andrew Niccol

This film depicts a biopunk vision of a future society driven by eugenics, where children are conceived through genetic manipulation to ensure they possess the best hereditary traits of their parents.

The exteriors and some interiors of the Gattaca complex were shot at Frank Lloyd Wright's Marin County Civic Centre (which also featured in *THX 1138*). The exterior of the protagonist Vincent Freeman's house was filmed at CLA Building, California State Polytechnic University, Pomona (Antoine Predock, 1993). The role of Wright's building, as the HQ of a futuristic aerospace corporation, has a certain irony, as it was completed in 1957.

1997

The Matrix
dir. Larry and Andy Wachowski *

In this vision of a distorted future 'reality' for most humans is actually simulated within 'the Matrix'. The protagonist, Neo, discovers the truth and joins a rebellion against the machines. Much of the film was shot in Sydney but avoided recognisable buildings to give the impression of an American, contemporary, high-rise city.

This film is less one for architecture fans than for typography geeks. In the green colour of early computer monitors, code in a custom typeface, designed by Simon Whiteley, regularly flows across the screen.

*Now known as Lana and Lilly Wachowski or 'The Wachowskis'.

1999

Futurama
30th Century Fox Television

Matt Groening, the creator of the longest running animated series in TV history, *The Simpsons*, named his animated science fiction series in honour of the 1939 New York World's Fair's Futurama (a huge diorama by Norman Bel Geddes).

Set in New New York in the 31st century, the city sits on top of Old New York which forms its sewage network. Themes under Groening's ironic lens include global warming and the state of the US city.

2002

Minority Report
dir. Steven Spielberg

In the year 2054, police apprehend criminals based on foreknowledge provided by three psychics called 'precogs'.

Spielberg wanted his imaginary future to seem viable. Thus familiar historic buildings in the Washington D.C. landscape are retained. The production designer, Alex McDowell, created sets which reflect much that was already happening in contemporary architecture, including curves and reflective cladding.

2003

Code 46
dir. Michael Winterbottom

This British science fiction love story created its various future city settings by filming in Shanghai, Dubai and Rajasthan. The world in the movie is divided between privileged 'insiders' who live within high density cities and 'outsiders' who cannot access city life. There are analogies between this totalitarian world and those depicted in *1984* and *Logan's Run*.

2005

Doctor Who
BBC

In one of the most heralded returns in television history, *Doctor Who*'s revival by Russell T Davies gave Christopher Eccleston the keys to the TARDIS. In the years since, Eccleston was succeeded by David Tennant and Matt Smith. Thanks to an increased budget and computer-generated effects, a large number of alien worlds and future cities have been realised over the years of the show.

Since the show was relaunched, it has become one of the BBC's biggest international hits, now shown in over seventy countries. The fiftieth anniversary episode, *The Day of the Doctor*, was simulcast in 94 countries, and shown in cinemas across the globe.

Three spin-offs have followed, *Torchwood* in 2006, *The Sarah Jane Adventures* (starring Elisabeth Sladen, assistant to Tom Baker's Doctor in the 'classic' series) in 2007, and *Class* in 2016, by 'young adult' writer Patrick Ness. The tenth series of the revived show, starring Peter Capaldi, will be broadcast in 2017.

2005

Aeon Flux
dir. Karyn Kusama

Aeon Flux, released in 2005, made use of Berlin's Treptow Crematorium (Shultes Frank Architeckten, 1998), the Tierheim Animal Shelter (Dietrich Bangert, 2002) and the Bauhaus Archive (original design Walter Gropius, 1964, building as realised in 1979 adapted by Alex Crijanovic and Hans Bandel) to create a home for a future utopian society - glossy and calm on the outside but greatly troubled beneath the surface.

The director originally wanted to film her future city of Bregna in Brasilia, the capital of Brazil. Practical considerations made Berlin a more viable option. The simplicity of the buildings was emphasised to create a sense of artificial calm within a manipulative manufactured society. The absence of clutter and disorder here becomes not calming but unnerving. Its real world settings and the solidity of these structures gives credibility to Aeon Flux's world.

2008

Fringe
Fox

JJ Abrams' *Fringe* broadcast on Fox in the US. The spiritual successor to *The X-Files*, an FBI team uses fringe science and forensic techniques to investigate a series of unexplained, often ghastly occurrences, which are related to mysteries surrounding a parallel universe and alternate timelines.

Fringe's story arc includes an alternate version of New York, slightly different to the familiar, with the alternative universe Manhatan more advanced technologically and still featuring the World Trade Centre's twin towers, and a bronze Statue of Liberty (rather than patinated-copper).

2009

Avatar
dir. James Cameron

Humans are colonising Pandora, a lush habitable moon of a gas giant, to mine the mineral unobtanium. The mining colony threatens the existence of a local humanoid species, the Na'vi.

Cameron wrote, directed, produced and co-edited his epic, having spent several years waiting for Computer Generated Imagery (CGI) technology to catch up with his vision. The film draws upon and references a huge number of science fiction books and films as well as the adventure fiction of Edgar Rice Burroughs and Rider Haggard. It remains the highest grossing film of all time with at least two sequels in the pipeline.

Moon
dir. Duncan James

The film follows a man who experiences a personal crisis nearing the end of his three-year solitary stint mining helium-3 on the far side of the moon.

This relatively low budget movie drew upon late seventies science fiction to create the bleak environment within which its protagonist undertakes his voyage of self-discovery – discovering various other selves in the process.

District 9
dir. Neill Blomkamp

Inspired by events in District Six, Cape Town during the apartheid era, the film depicts xenophobia and social segregation in an alien refugee camp.

Shot on location in Soweto the film reveals its narrative in a 'found footage' format. Interviews, surveillance camera video and news clips relay the story of the forced relocation of a population of aliens from one government camp to another. The reaction of the human population against the segregated minority explores the central theme, using 'speciesism' as an allegory for racism.

2009

Star Trek
dir. **JJ Abrams**

In this *Star Trek* rebot, Chris Pine and Zachary Quinto take on the challenging roles of Kirk and Spock. Although the film is a prequel to the narrative of the first TV series its set and technology were updated to overcome the kitsch quality of the dated original. The production designer Scott Chambliss acknowledged the Catalan architect Antoni Gaudi as the inspiration for the curving and exoskeletal elements of his new starship.

Two further films have followed, 2013's *Star Trek Into Darkness* (dir. JJ Abrams) and 2016's *Star Trek Beyond* (dir. Justin Lin).

2010

Inception
dir. **Christopher Nolan**

A professional thief who steals information from his victim's subconscious is offered the chance to have his criminal history erased if he can implant an idea into the subconscious mind of his target.

The film's locations and the distortion of its architecture, including compression, folding and explosive destruction, demanded a huge budget and led to the development of new filming techniques. Tokyo, London, Paris, Tangeir, Los Angeles and Alberta reflected the infinite architectural forms of the dream sequences which are at the core of the film.

2012

The Hunger Games
dir. **Gary Ross**

The first of four films based on the young-adult novels by Suzanne Collins. Set in the dystopian future nation of Panem, young people try to survive a fight to the death in a televised event.

While most of the action takes place within a, more or less natural (but camera filled) wooded landscape, the giant, sculptural, 'cornucopia' plays a key role. In the original book the cornucopia (Latin for horn of plenty) which provides both weapons and shelter for the protagonists is golden. In the films it is a silver or grey metal form, derivative in its jointed planar form of the architecture of Frank Gehry.

2012

Dredd
dir. Pete Travis

Judge Dredd (Karl Urban) is a law enforcer given the power of judge, jury and executioner in Mega-City One, a vast, dystopian city in a post-apocalyptic wasteland.

The action takes place in the, ironically titled, Peach Trees, a 200-storey tower block slum ruled by a vicious female drug lord known as Ma-Ma. As with so many science fiction films the de-humanising city gone wrong bears a remarkable resemblance to a high-rise American metropolis.

2013

Gravity
dir. Alfonso Cuarón

Sandra Bullock and George Clooney are astronauts stranded in space after the mid-orbit destruction of their space shuttle. This British-American film was shot in the UK, with the exception of the final landing scene which was filmed at Lake Powell, Arizona. Although its narrative frame is science fiction this is very much an 'individual against all the odds' tale.

2013

Elysium
dir. Neill Blomkamp

With its action taking place on a ravaged planet Earth and the eponymous luxurious space colony of Elysium the film explores political themes of social class, health care and urban sustainability.

Filmed in Mexico and Vancouver, while the movie's thrust is critical of the urban condition, highlighting its counterpoints of rural poverty and worker exploitation, it also portrays the potential of the contemporary city to provide a quality of life to which many would aspire.

2014

Interstellar
dir. Christopher Nolan

Yet another space based narrative – the inevitable frontier of the post-2000 sci-fi movie, *Interstellar* follows a crew of volunteers through a wormhole near Saturn as they journey to a distant galaxy. The film uses effects developed on Nolan's earlier movie, *Inception*.

2015

The Martian
dir. Ridley Scott

An astronaut (Matt Damon) is left for dead on Mars. He manages to return to the deserted base. The film follows his struggle for survival and the efforts of others, on Earth, to rescue him.

Again in this film a 'lost in space' scenario is the premise for an individual struggle for survival against the odds – a Robinson Crusoe story for the space age.

BIBLIOGRAPHY

Print

Bell, James, *Sci-Fi: Days of Fear and Wonder*, BFI Publishing, 2014

Grant, Barry Keith, *100 Science Fiction Films (Screen Guides)*, BFI Publishing, 2014

Haley, Guy, *Sci-Fi Chronicles: A Visual History of the Galaxy's Greatest Science Fiction*, Aurum Press, 2014

Websites and webpages

archigram.westminster.ac.uk

imdb.com

wikipedia.org

www.fulltable.com/vts/f/fut/menu.htm

sciencefictionruminations.wordpress.com/egregious-science-fiction-cover-art/

exhibitions.guggenheim.org/futurism/architecture

ACKNOWLEDGEMENTS

The exhibition, *Adventures in Space*, a key event in the year-long, Scotland-wide, Festival of Architecture programme was a popular draw at Glasgow's Lighthouse from July until September 2016. Jon Jardine, as curator, commissioned over 190 original drawings for that show, which are reproduced in this volume, alongside a number of additional architectural images.

Jon would like to extend particular thanks to Carol-Ann Hildersley for her help and unstinting patience through the gestation of this publication, to artists Ian Stuart Campbell, Douglas Prince, Ciana Pullen and Piotr Sell and to his ever supportive partner, Brendan Nash.

INDEX